"Good morning, Miss Minturn," said a voice just behind her. "Taking an admiring look at your home?"

"What?" Theodora turned, astonished, for she had not thought to see Lord Bourne again.

"I have come for you. We are going to have a talk." He was maneuvering his big horse close to her filly. Then he was touching on the left, one arm reached out and around her waist, the other caught her under the legs and she was lifted and swung across the saddle in front of him. He settled her so she leaned against his shoulder. When she started up to protest, she was pulled back again.

"Stay still. I'm taking you for that talk I am due."

"But . . .," she gasped, "what a romantic fashion to do it."

THEODORA

by

Caroline Arnett

A FAWCETT CREST BOOK

Fawcett Books, Greenwich, Connecticut

THEODORA

A Fawcett Crest Book printed by arrangement with
Harold Ober Associates.

ISBN: 0-449-23347-2

Printed in the United States of America

10 9 8 7 6 5 4 3 2 1

THEODORA

One

IN THE library of the Tudor section of Ardsley Hall, Miss Theodora Minturn and Myles Chilcot, Lord Deveron, looked at each other with scarcely concealed dislike. Even if they had not been coheirs, they would not at that moment have been drawn to each other. In the past three weeks neither had thought much about the coheir nor wondered what one was like, but neither had expected what each now confronted.

Mr. Tillingbourne, the lawyer, had introduced them all with a bright satisfaction and was now requesting tea of the butler and arranging that the two companions should be comfortable by the fire while he disclosed the terms of Lord Stanford's will to the heirs.

Astonishment and anticipation had been Miss Minturn's chief emotions during the interval between the arrival of the letter summoning her to Ardsley Hall and entering the place five minutes ago. The coheir, when her thoughts brushed the subject, would be, she assumed, a solid, sensible man, probably a little older than her own twenty years, who would be of calm assistance in this unusual situation. Instead she was regarding one of the handsomest men she had ever seen—thick dark hair, heavy eyelashes hiding the eyes above a straight nose, and firm chin. The quiet good taste of his country clothes indicated a gentleman of the first stare. He had just now looked at her through his quizzing glass, dropped it, and turned away in a manner that betokened complete distaste. How would she be able to share the Hall with a pink of the ton?

Lord Deveron had seen in his one sweeping glance a thin girl, neither short nor tall, with badly cut brown hair, and clad in a plain round dress of blue serge, who had every appearance of having just emerged from the school room. Without much thought to the matter he had assumed his coheir would be someone knowledgeable and of a certain distinction. How could he rub along on equal terms, living on a large estate with a dowdy chit like this? At least, however, she would be submissive and follow whatever directions he might decide to give.

"Miss Minturn, my lord, tea will be brought quickly for Mrs. Farraby and Mr. Gifford, but would you not prefer to proceed directly to the discussion of Lord Stanford's will?" The stocky, gray-haired lawyer beamed as he moved to the heirs who were allowing the footmen to assist in removing cloak and coat.

"Oh, the will for us by all means," Thea said in a clear voice as she untied the ribbons of her bonnet and ran her fingers through her hair, forgetting that was no longer a suitable gesture for her. "Having heard it, we will then need the tea to help us to recover from whatever are the provisions."

"Certainly, the will," agreed Lord Deveron languidly. "We are to sit at the table, I take it?"

Thea had also noticed the three arm chairs drawn to the round table in front of the bay windows and moved quickly to take the one which had its back to the light, something she had learned when explaining their misdemeanors to the flighty young ladies of Miss Whitwell's

Seminary in Bath. Lord Deveron inclined his head two inches as he pulled out the chair opposite, and Mr. Tillingbourne made something of a bow as he took the chair before a pile of papers.

"Before we commence," Thea began as firmly as if she were still instructing the young ladies, "I would like to thank you, Mr. Tillingbourne, for locating Mrs. Ferraby, whom Lord Stanford desired should become my companion for my journey here and for as long as she desires, and for the care and consideration you have shown us both. Sending the Ardsley coach for us, first to Swanage and then to Bath, and the arrangements made in advance for comfortable accommodations at the inns were greatly appreciated."

There was a confirming murmur from Mrs. Farraby; Mr. Gifford, introduced by Lord Deveron simply as his friend, said something about "must always look out for the comfort of ladies"; and Mr. Tillingbourne said he was happy the ladies had been pleased. Lord Deveron's voice cut through the sounds sharply. "That is all very well, admirable no doubt, but may we proceed to the business that brought us here?"

What an unpleasant man, thought Thea, with whom she must somehow share this Hall, and was pleased that his wish was defeated by the arrival of the tea for the other two. While waiting for the footmen to leave, she openly looked around the room. Someone had had the ancient panelling painted white and also the ceiling between the dark square beams. The draperies at the windows behind her were a figured red damask that went with the turkish rug on the floor, the gilded plaster cornucopias overflowing with red roses on the white marble pilasters at either side of the fireplace, and the uniform in the portrait above the mantel. There were crowded bookshelves on two walls; the small sofa and armchairs were upholstered in old-fashioned red leather, rather worn; and the whole air of the room was one of brightness and good cheer. It gave her hope that the rest of the mansion would be equally pleasing.

"As you know from my letters, Miss Minturn, Lord Deveron"— the lawyer's words drew Thea's wandering attention—"the late Lord Stanford made you his heirs in his last will drawn about a year ago."

Thea had intended to frame the question elegantly but she forgot. "Why us?" she asked eagerly.

The lawyer smiled benignly. "What I also asked, Miss Minturn. You are both only third cousins twice removed to his late lordship, though you are the closest of his remaining relations. There are several in the next degree. Dreadful how a family can die out, be killed off, so to speak, in the service of our country. . . . But to continue. He replied to my inquiry by telling me that you and your parents were the only ones who had never asked him for money, that when you each were nearly impoverished you had set about supporting yourselves, and that you each, on your one command visit here when very young, had displayed the most spirit. I might add that using your last money to buy a pair of colors and rising in rank in the army was in your favor, my lord, though inheriting the title and competence from a relative on the other side almost worked against you. But the fact that no landed estate went with your title, and that his title ended with his death, seemed in the end a fortunate combination to Lord Stanford. Since you, and the other surviving cousins, are descended from female lines, it has taken time to discover you, though I have found a few letters that are of some assistance. I agreed with Lord Stanford that his reasons for selecting you were excellent. His two sons were killed in the wars, you know, and then, a few years ago, his only grandson, All this is merely to answer Miss Minturn's quite proper question."

"Fascinating," murmured Lord Deveron, obviously not

meaning it at all. "Why we are here . . . But there are conditions?"

"Yes, my lord. Ardsley Hall, as you have not had an opportunity to observe, is a large mansion built in three periods, the last two utilizing the stones of the first, the original castle. On either side of the gatehouse, which is all that remains of that castle, lie the two wings. The one in which we are now was built in the Elizabethan period. It was used by the family for more than a hundred years, with one-half the original castle left closed and standing. Then a bride, a rich heiress, desired a mansion more in the mode of her own time, so the other half of the castle was pulled down and used to construct the second wing in the Palladian style. The Tudor wing was preserved for the Dowager, who refused to have a Dower house built for her as was customary. Both wings have been used by the family, by sons when they married, once by a daughter, for guests. Each Lord Stanford resided in the new wing until the last, his late lordship, who preferred this one. Each wing is of course complete, furnished in appropriate fashion, with all domestic offices, designed to accommodate large families. But, as I said, wars . . . fevers. . . ." He gestured with one hand. "Lord Stanford was the last of his line. Since there were to be two heirs, strangers, he ordered that the Palladian wing be opened on his death, put in order, and a complete staff engaged for whichever of you two preferred it."

She was staring at him as if he were a fortuneteller, Thea realized, and looked away. Lord Deveron was lounging in the chair he had pushed back from the table, one hand dangling his quizzing glass. By the fireplace Mrs. Farraby was telling Mr. Gifford something of their travels while he listened seriously and ate his way through a plate of little cakes. As he halted, Mr. Tillingbourne looked sad for a moment, then recommenced briskly. "You are each of you left an amount of money which has already been settled in a trust to provide you a small yearly income; the amounts I will communicate privately."

"How thoughtful of him," breathed Thea.

"He was determined that Ardsley should again be a home for families," the lawyer went on, acknowledging Thea's words with a slight inclination. "You therefore will share the estate, one in one wing, one in the other. The stables, gardens, park are to be shared jointly. I, that is the estate, will pay all costs. But you are only to enjoy the amenities of Ardsley for six months, unless some conditions are fulfilled. Also, Stanford House on Cavendish Square in London is at the disposal of Miss Minturn for that period of time. But," he held up one hand, "you might both be heirs in perpetuity if you each marry within the six-month period. Lord Stanford was not a patient man, you understand, and wished everything to be set in motion as soon as possible."

"But that is infamous," stammered Thea. "I have no intention of marrying." And hated herself as she said it for it gave Deveron the opportunity to cast her a look that practically said "of course." She didn't need that look to tell her she was no beauty and resented the fact that he was so handsome he would find no difficulty in obtaining a bride.

"As I indicated, ma'am, Lord Stanford wished Ardsley Hall filled with children as soon as possible."

Her next question was obvious. "If each of us is not married at the end of six months, what then?"

"There are two cousins whose parents applied only twice for help to Lord Stanford. He believed they might be the next most worthy. I am engaged in discovering them. They will inherit under the same conditions as you. If they fail, or do not in my opinion qualify for Ardsley, there are two more. If they are not available, the Hall will become an endowed school for boys, sons of noncommissioned officers of His Majesty's army. Lord Stanford's

first concern was the family and the Hall, as you understand, but the army was also of importance to him."

"It's a damned queer will," remarked Lord Deveron,
twirling his glass.

"You might say it is unusual and individual, as was
Lord Stanford himself." The rebuke was gentle, but it
was there. "However, there is one other condition by
which you might become permanent heirs whether or
not you marry. That is if either of you find the Zamora
emeralds which are then to be devoted to increasing the
wealth and consequence of the family."

"Ah, yes," said Mrs. Farraby from beside the tea table.
"You had better recount the tale, sir, for the young
people will not have heard it."

Mr. Tillingbourne shoved his chair a little to one side
so he could speak to all. "The story of the Zamora
emeralds is the most famous of the family tales. . . .

"At the time of James I, the then Stanford, Richard,
was a baronet. To improve the family standing and
fortunes he outfitted his own ship, as had so many of
his compatriots, intent on plundering the Spanish gal-
leons returning from their wealthy colonies in South
America and almost invariably bearing treasure. Richard's
father had spent much of the family fortunes building this
wing and in unwise speculations. Richard and his ship
did well, capturing several Spanish vessels of adequate
size whose cargoes could be sold and whose captives
ransomed.

"On his last voyage he came upon a galleon disabled
by a storm, boarded her with a little difficulty, found her
hold worth ransacking and also leaking. Among the
wealthy passengers was the daughter of the president, or
governor, of New Granada, now Colombia, returning to
her family in Spain for her wedding. Richard transferred
the more wealthy of the passengers to his own ship, as
much of the valuables in the hold as could be saved, the

not inconsiderable treasure the galleon carried, and left it to sink with what remained of crew and passengers. Isabella Maria, he announced, was his own private property for her ransom would be very large. Accompanied by an aged aunt as duenna, she had brought as part of her dowry a massive set of emeralds—necklace, bracelets, earrings—the stones, large and pure, were from the mines of New Granada.

"At Plymouth he made the arrangements about captives, cargo, crew, and ship, and then brought Isabella Maria here to Ardsley Hall. For most of the time she was confined in the tower of the gatehouse just behind us. It was said he was in love with her but more in love with the gold she would bring and with the emeralds, which he took in charge. Though she was not cossetted, she was not harmed. He sent word to her family in Spain and named her ransom. The elderly aunt died. No one could speak Spanish. Isabella refused to learn English, though she did permit her portrait to be painted, since she could hardly refuse. Then a cousin arrived with the ransom, demanding girl and emeralds. He was allowed to see Isabella but was informed that the emeralds, by right of capture, would remain with Richard. The cousin took up the sack of gold and left."

There was no sound in the room. The lawyer paused a moment as if for breath, then resumed.

"He returned that moonlit night when all were asleep except Isabella. Someone had been well bribed, for she walked proudly out of the door beside the tower and across to the rider on the black horse. The cousin gave a shout that woke Richard. He rushed to the window to see Isabella swung up to the saddle. The cousin looked at Richard in the window, held up the sack of gold and poured it, a shining stream in the moonlight, on to the ground with a gesture of contempt, laughed, and rode away. Richard, when he told the story, held he had the last laugh, though he had had it in mind to increase the ransom, for he had the emeralds as well as the gold. The only thing for which she had ever pleaded was her jewels; each time he laughed and refused; each time she wept bitterly."

Mr. Tillingbourne paused again. "You must forgive the extravagance of the tale and the manner of telling, but that is how it has come down. Richard put the gold to good use. He redecorated this wing, took over a good farm, and entered on some profitable trading ventures. Sometime later, he was granted a peerage, and shortly thereafter he acquired a wife who had a modest fortune of her own and whose father wished a title in the family.

"Once his wife wore the emeralds to a ball at court and they were deemed unusually fine though she did not wear them well, being blonde and frail. Only a few days after their return here two masked robbers were discovered in the baron's bedroom when he and his wife returned early from dinner at a neighbor's. The men had crowbars and were prying the safe from the wall. Richard shouted for the footmen and the miscreants were routed, fleeing by the window they had broken. It was said Richard decided that the risks of displaying the emeralds in order to add to his consequence were not worth the worry and trouble of guarding them. He sent his wife to stay with her mother, ordered the servants from the house for a week, and when all returned announced that the Zamora emeralds were hidden so safely they could never be found until he revealed the secret to his son. That he had no chance to do for he broke his neck out hunting. The emeralds have never been seen again."

"Sounds like a fairy tale from a nurse, only no fairies," exclaimed Mr. Gifford.

"There have been attempts to find them—by robbers, that is—for of course the family has searched, but there has been no success and no clues," Mr. Tillingbourne added with finality.

"Suppose they were found by some one other than the —er—heirs?" Lord Deveron asked without much interest.

Mr. Tillingbourne spread his hands. "Exactly my question. Lord Stanford laughed. He could not believe his heirs would be more stupid than other people and, if they are to be found, it will be by one of his family, but I am convinced he did not believe they would be. You will find portraits of the two ladies of this tale in the Long Gallery." Again he halted and looked from Thea to Deveron. "With the explanations you have heard, are you, Miss Minturn, and you, Lord Deveron, prepared to accept the legacies of Lord Stanford under the conditions laid down in his will? Or would you prefer a little time to think it over?"

Thea had no doubts. Six months at Ardsley as coheir —why, anything might happen! And there was the trust fund. However, small, it would be of the greatest importance to her in the future since she had been compelled to leave Miss Whitwell's to come to Ardsley. Lord Deveron's situation was different, but even a noble lord would not disdain any addition to his estate. "I hold it is an improbable, unbelievable will in many aspects, but I accept," she announced in the most positive tones she could muster.

"No need to make a proclamation of it, Miss—er— Minturn." One lifted eyebrow showed his lordship's boredom but his direct glance, the first she had exchanged, surprised her for his eyes were very blue. Her chief emotion, however, was envy of his eyelashes for hers were short and thick and could not be admired. "I am sure we are sharing a variety of emotions, ma'am," he went on, "but you can set your mind at rest. I also accept, Mr. Tillingbourne."

"Good." The lawyer looked as pleased as if the inheritance was his own. "May I felicitate you both? You have your boxes and are prepared to move in as of this day? Then we must settle how the Hall is to be divided between you."

"Pretty unusual that, dividing a house," objected Mr. Gifford. "Never heard of it. Not sure it's done."

"It will be here," the lawyer said shortly.

"And that monstrous square thing we came in, gatehouse, is it? Looks as old as Adam's rib."

"It is all that remains of the original castle and was retained, I must admit, out of pride, to show how long the family had held the estate."

There was no languor about Lord Deveron as he straightened. "If agreeable, I will take the newer wing. Miss Cordelia Albury has driven over to inspect the place. She prefers it to the earlier." ·

"She would," exclaimed Thea with a touch of amusement.

"You are acquainted with Miss Albury?" There was extreme doubt in his question.

"Oh, yes," Thea told him composedly. "We have been introduced several times over the last two years in the Pump Room at Bath. She does not remember me." As she said it she knew he was thinking it was no wonder she escaped the mind of a young lady of fashion, and she wished she had not added those last words.

"She is an Accredited Beauty," he went on, with enthusiasm.

"Indeed she is so held by those who admire marble," Thea agreed cordially and felt a tiny touch of triumph at the gasp from Mr. Gifford.

"Would you not care to return to the front oval of the driveway from which both wings may be seen?" Mr. Tillingbourne asked quickly. "Miss Minturn, as the lady, really has the first choice. Or would you care to walk through both of the wings before reaching a decision?"

An inspection of all the rooms might be enlightening, but it would take a great deal of time. Thea knew her mind was already made up and felt it fortunate she and Miss Albury did not have the same tastes. She rose quickly. "Let us go to the front driveway. There was no way to see the entire Hall from the coach."

Mr. Tillingbourne went to open the door and guide her through the vestibule into the oblong stone hall beyond. In spite of small windows cut in the walls, the place was dim and strange for each side was a copy of the other. First came the vestibule behind the huge door, with a small door cut into it at each side, then the vestibule between two large entrances to long halls. Beyond them rose wide stairways to the first floor to halt at another hall, and next to them towered a blackened fireplace. Two windows showed space and lawn. Thea halted and looked up the four floors to a much too small skylight. "Since we are to divide the Hall in two, would it not be well to put a wall through here?" She felt the need to say something, and it was the first that occurred to her. "The way from one wing to another is quite open, and there is the danger the two families might live in each other's pockets."

"I hardly think there is danger of that," Lord Deveron said crisply and impatiently headed for the door.

"You are right in that there is no hindrance of going from one wing to the other," Mr. Tillingbourne agreed, "but this entrance need not be used for there is a doorway on each front and of course others at the sides and back."

By this time a footman was holding open the door, and Thea stepped down a few steps, across a parterre, down again to the long oval of gravel, and turned to look at Ardsley Hall. Her gasp apparently gratified Mr. Tillingbourne. Deveron did not even raise his glass.

"I say, it's big," announced Mr. Gifford who had come

to rest at his side. "Not like Blenheim or Hardwick, but big."

"And unusual," added Mrs. Farraby gently.

They were facing the gatehouse, high and medieval. To the right extended the Tudor wing, uneven, two jutting bays, a doorway not centered, wide windows on three stories, and sturdy yellow chimneys above the sloping roof. To the left stretched the later section, flat-faced but for a small porch with free-standing Doric pillars, long narrow windows framed by Doric pilasters, all dignified and uncompromising even to the slender chimneys above the shallow roof. All they had in common was that they were made from the same gray stone.

"As I said," Mr. Tillingbourne took up, "each house is furnished appropriately and is staffed, and each has a wing at the back at right angles to form the court, with flower gardens beyond the yew hedge that bounds that. The stables, paddock, gardens, greenhouse, and cottages are to the rear. I must tell you that nothing is to be changed during the time of trial." He stopped, waited a minute, then rather pointedly addressed Thea. "Do you believe you can reach a decision now as to which of the houses you prefer, Miss Minturn?"

Thea nodded. "Indeed I can, the older one. And that is so fortunate for it agrees with Lord Deveron's desire," she added sweetly.

"Fortunate indeed," he drawled, half turning away. "It would have been yet another awkwardness to have to come to points within the first hour." He glanced toward the westering sun. "I take it there is nothing more to be discussed at the moment, Mr. Tillingbourne? Then pray forgive me now."

Looking faintly surprised, the lawyer glanced at Thea, who shook her head. "Very well, of course. I will come and meet you tomorrow morning at ten to go over the properties, as is customary, as if your inheritance is final."

"Very good." Lord Deveron bent his head to Mrs. Farraby and Thea. "Until tomorrow . . . an engagement. . . . "

"Tea and dinner with Miss Albury and her family," explained Mr. Gifford happily to Mrs. Farraby. "Can't miss that, you know, or be late. Their place, Casons, not four miles distant. Look forward to tomorrow, ma'am, Miss Minturn," and he loped after the tall figure striding toward the left-hand mansion.

"Are their senses quite disturbed?" Thea asked in bewilderment. "What a curious way to behave."

"No. They are merely two gentlemen in love with a Beauty and not permitting anything to keep them from her side," Mrs. Farraby explained with amusement. "Do you not agree, Mr. Tillingbourne? Miss Minturn, neither of you have had tea. May we not return to the house for some refreshment which I am persuaded you would both find welcome."

It was so welcome that over it the lawyer relaxed his formal manner. "You have two treasures in your butler and housekeeper, Brewton and his wife," he told Thea, "and," taking another cake, "an excellent cook. The Brewtons are second generation with the family and are informed and devoted."

"None of this seems real." Thea shook her head. "There was no time to grow accustomed to the change, and perhaps that is as well, since it apparently will not be for long."

"Then this is the time to tell you the further provision of his lordship's will in your regard." He settled more comfortably in his chair, and the brown eyes beamed. "It seems when he was young he admired your grandmother and took a little more interest in you than in the others. He said you showed, on that one call, that you were an independent little thing, which meant you were as proud as all your family. He was well aware a penniless girl in this world has no future, so he set up a trust fund to be managed by a bank in London for you and your heirs that will pay you a thousand pounds a year which would be useful, no matter what your condition, but is not sufficient to attract fortune hunters."

"How very kind," Thea stammered. "I had no idea . . ."

"He was pleased with his thought and knew you would be grateful. Furthermore, as I said, the townhouse, which is not large, is at your disposal for the six months with the expenses, as well as your own, paid by the estate. It was his hope you would remove to London and enjoy the Season."

"Again, so kind," but that was said thoughtfully. "The purpose is for me to find a husband, I take it?"

"To be bald about it, yes. His lordship held that all attractive girls of good family should be married and that opportunity should be put in your way, for your own sake and for the sake of Ardsley. Send me word when you wish to go, and I will arrange all."

"I seem to be able to say nothing but 'how kind.'" Her smile was troubled. "I am not accustomed to this way of living, you know."

"But it is in your blood, and you have Mrs. Farraby to sustain you. I know his lordship hoped you would enjoy these months, no matter what the outcome." He rose. "Remember I wish to assist you in any way possible. Now I will instruct Mrs. Brewton to come and make herself known to you. And," as he bowed a little, "may your first night at Ardsley Hall, and all others, be exceedingly pleasant."

A comfortable Mrs. Brewton presented herself and conducted them to their rooms on the first floor. Thea's was large and panelled but made bright by the yellow-and-white patterned curtains and draperies, put in by his late lordship to relieve the gloom. It was the room of the master, and had once even been Sir Richard's. Left alone, Thea sat down quickly on the window bench. Her life had been simple—with her parents, schools, these last two years as a combination instructress and governess at Miss Whitwell's. No wonder she felt subdued, by the place, by the people, by what the months might bring. That realization was annoying and lowering to the spirits. She must bring herself about and owned she had no idea how to do so.

Two

AT THE close of the light supper of jellied chicken, poached trout, peas from the greenhouse, and an assortment of creams and cakes, Thea sent her compliments to the cook. Supper had been served in the morning room, a corner room hung with cheerful landscape-printed linen from France, and which lay beyond the formal dining room. Thea and Mrs. Farraby had exchanged innocuous observations of life in rural England, and as they rose agreed a coze in the library would be agreeable.

They strolled back through the rooms instead of following the corridor which, with windows giving on the central court, stretched the length of the house. On the way they paused to admire the rather hearty yellow of the draperies and fruit decorating the panels in the dining room and the green of the saloon, where the panels were enhanced by flowers also done in raised plaster and painted in the manner introduced under Elizabeth by the first wave of Italian workmen, and the marble fireplace surmounted by a frieze of deer.

"Obviously some healthy gentlemen have been responsible for the decor," observed Mrs. Farraby, "but it is very relaxing for there is no need to express appreciation."

Thea agreed and added that of all the rooms she preferred the library, for it was intended to be bright and comfortable and succeeded to admiration. Here two armchairs were drawn before a small fire. Mrs. Farraby settled in one. "There is nothing so gratifying as a well-run household, which I must say this is; and it is evident you will not need to order a meal, and any preference you express will be gratified. Now, we are prepared to talk and to listen. I vow I am hard put to it to know which I prefer. It is my suggestion we each reveal enough of our lives to apprise the other of how we come to be here at this moment. I must say I find you a pretty-behaved girl, and I am convinced we will deal well together, but it is always so helpful to know a little about one's friends. Do you not agree?"

She looked across to Thea, her head of gray curls slightly atilt, her large brown eyes inquiring and kindly. "To begin with," she went on, "do you feel you could bring yourself to call me Cousin Susan? It would be so much less formal. Do you feel you might tell me a little of yourself . . . as little as you wish?"

"Dear ma'am," Thea leaned forward eagerly, "I know I am most fortunate that Lord Stanford suggested you accompany me. I will be happy to call you Cousin Susan. I feel already we are friends and I know that I am going to need your support and guidance."

"Not as much as you now think." There came a small chuckle. "You have been behaving quite properly. But, to begin with, do you know aught of this Lord Deveron?"

"No. My parents were not in touch with any of their families, which were small and scattered. From the document I was sent, it seems his name is Myles Chilcot, and the title and a pleasant competence came quite unexpectedly from a cousin on his father's side."

"Surprises are seldom so welcome . . . . Even if we had not been told we would have known from his manner that he was a military man. We know nothing of Mr. Gifford, but his role seems to me to be that of Greek chorus—though perhaps I flatter him. You will never be any kind of a chorus, my love. Did you know anything of your third cousin twice removed?"

Thea began to laugh. "Indeed, no, Cousin Susan. Once when we were running close to the wind—for my father, you must know, was an officer in the navy until wounded and retired at half-pay and we had no resources—he and mother amused themselves discussing a distant cousin of great wealth who knew as little of them as they of him, and spent an hour recalling a very brief visit to his estate and wondering how our lack of one could be brought to his attention. But in the end they agreed that even the most romantic method, having mother somehow frighten the horses of his coach so my father could rush out and halt them and rescue a grateful lordship, would possesss too great an air of contrivance, and that for even five hundred pounds they would not toadeat a noble lord. So you see I was brought up to ask for no help from anyone."

"Your childhood, however, was happy?" Mrs. Farraby asked gently.

"Oh, exceedingly." Thea watched a little flame change from blue to red. "Or it was except when mother followed father when his ship was sent overseas and I was put in school in France and then in Bath. Those five years, after he retired, were so very happy; I was called a merry child. My mother and father, you see, were so handsome and enjoyed and loved each other so much that sometimes they would just sit and look at each other and burst out laughing, or dance, or sing, and then snatch me up to join them and tell me I would grow up more charming than both together and finally marry a fairy prince. It was my father who insisted I must be called Thea as it was a more attractive name for a girl than the usual Theo. Fortunately, in those years my mother's one-time nanny was with us and she removed notions from my imaginings and pointed out that with my coloring I could never approach the beauty of my parents, so I must instead learn to be sensible and practical and make the most of whatever good qualities I might discover in myself. Good advice that turned out to be, for brown hair and hazel eyes have never been held in high esteem and it is as well I learned early I would never be a beauty before my parents quite spoiled me."

"But what happened, my child?"

Thea left her chair and went to look out the bay window to the far hills fading into the dusk. It was still difficult to talk about her parents without that dreadful feeling of loss and sadness flooding over her for a moment. But, as always, she conquered it and went back to her chair. "We lived in a tiny cottage on the coast of Devon, near the water, which we all loved. One morning we took some bread and cheese to a small beach for a swim and nuncheon and found the rug we used to lie on had been forgotten. So I hurried back to our cottage, a ten-minute walk. It was a sunny, blue day. They must have been lured into the water. When I returned they were not on the beach, only shoes and outer garments and the food. I called. I swam along the shore, around the point of rocks. Then I ran for help. The fishermen were concerned, for we were great favorites. But they were never found. It was held one of them must have caught a chill, a cramp, the other had gone to help, and both were pulled down by an undertow, or an offshore current."

"And then?"

Thea took a deep breath. The worst was over. "My father's pension ceased, of course. I sold what I could and wrote to Miss Whitwell to apply for a place, for it was there I had spent two years while my father was in the West Indies Squadron and my mother lived in Jamaica. I had learned much of manners and comportment, just living with my parents. Also they taught me history, light mathematics, drawing and coloring with water paints, something of spheres and globes—both terrestrial and celestial, and improved my French. I confess I am sadly deficient in music, but Miss Whitwell overlooked that and hired me as a junior mistress. And there, but for Lord Stanford, I should have spent my life."

"That I am inclined to doubt, but how fortunate he rescued you. Your position must have been tiring, for you are far too thin. A few weeks of proper food will work wonders for you. But, pray tell me how you came to the Pump Room at Bath?"

"Because I would escort the girls, some of whom were allowed to go on occasion, or accompany their families. On my father's side I am a cousin of Lord Minturn, and we have met, but he has five daughters to marry off, and I could not apply to him for assistance."

"Of course not." Mrs. Farraby used the poker on the fire for a moment. "You have contrived admirably to provide for yourself and deserve any good fortune that may come your way. I hope for you."

"As I do for myself," Thea agreed, cheerful again. "But, if you do not object, ma'am, how are we cousins?"

"Distant . . . your grandmother on the Leighton side was a cousin of my mother, which Stanford must have discovered. I encountered him several times in India, but he was too casual an acquaintance for me to turn to him for aid, and in truth there was no need. My dear husband left me enough to live on if I am careful, and I am long accustomed to that. For I eloped, I must tell you, during my First Season and never regretted it. My family did not approve of a younger son with no expectations except what he could make of the army, but my mother never referred to me as Barracks Sue—as did one duchess annoyed at her daughter who eloped with a young officer. My James did well and there was a small inheritance; and then came a fever, and so I was left alone with a cottage in Dorset, and there I have lived ever since. Oh, it has been agreeable enough, but I never could become sufficiently attached to flowers or birds or any of the other pursuits considered suitable for aging ladies. So I was overjoyed at Mr. Tillingbourne's letter and offer to join you. And I must repeat that I am sure we will deal admirably together."

"And enjoy whatever befalls us," Thea added blithely and sent for the tea table.

Thea found the tour the next morning vaguely uncomfortable. Though all the staff were undoubtedly acquainted with the will of his late lordship, Thea and Deveron were treated with the courtesy they would have encountered if they had been the permanent heirs, for which Thea was grateful. She and Deveron ignored each other and indeed had no occasion to converse. She knew she had drawn his attention when she exclaimed with delight at the gray filly, named Dawn, provided for her and had probably shocked him by her old worn riding habit. But there was no occasion even to glance at him as Mr. Tillingbourne escorted them around the boundaries of the estate. When the tour of the stables, cottages and farms was over, Deveron excused himself abruptly, for which she almost thanked him as she was spared the need to be polite and invite him to luncheon. Mr. Tillingbourne, however, was happy to remain and proved an agreeable guest, entertaining the ladies with tales of the countryside. Strolling down the hall to the gatehouse, he pointed out a small room at the end opposite the library, which was the office of the estate manager, but was also available for Thea's use at any time.

As they reached the high stone hall, there was a commotion in the opposite doorway. A vision—no other word was possible—in a simple dress of pink twill, a blue scarf becomingly draped, with golden curls caught in a blue ribbon, and an alabaster complexion and blue eyes, emerged with Deveron at her side. Followed by Mr. Gifford and a blond young man, they strolled across the flagging with complete insouciance. For a moment Thea seethed at their calm asssumption they were welcome, but she knew she must assert her position and that fury would show a want of conduct. She advanced, not too quickly, and held out her hand. "Miss Albury! How very kind of you to come to call so quickly!"

The other's hand rose slowly and Thea found the startled look in the blue eyes, which she had always held a little too small for real beauty, most gratifying. Deveron, evidently, had not thought to recall any encounters at Bath. She turned to her cousin. "Dear Mrs. Farraby, this is Miss Cordelia Albury who, I gather, lives nearby, and I am sure the gentleman we do not know is her brother, for the likeness is striking. And Mr. Tillingbourne you know, I am sure."

Mrs. Farraby bent her head a little. "So neighborly to come the first day," she murmured. "Good afternoon, gentlemen."

Thea realized she had not spoken to the men but did not rectify that omission for Miss Albury, recovered from her surprise, gave a gay little laugh. "We could hardly do other since dear Deveron had invited us to luncheon. It has been such a pleasure to go over the house he has so wisely chosen. It has great possibilities, and I have always yearned to do over completely in the newest fashion rooms of just that older style."

"I trust Lord Deveron explained that nothing can be sold from either for a certain period," Mr. Tillingbourne said flatly.

"Of course. But furniture can be moved out of the way to the attics." Miss Albury dismissed that problem. "Dear Miss Minturn. So fortunate to find you home. We have come to go over this quaint mansion that is your portion, for I vow I will not be happy until I have had a glimpse of it all."

"That is, if it is convenient." Deveron spoke quickly, but there was no doubt in his voice.

"You have come at the exact moment," Thea told the pink vision gaily. "I had just requested Mr. Tillingbourne to show us a few of the important rooms. I am sure he would not object to adding you to his audience." She was sure she could trust him to pick up his cue.

Mr. Tillingbourne gave a quarter bow. "It will be a pleasure to act as guide for you, Miss Minturn, though this visit will be only a survey; a thorough examination would require considerable time. I must add that Brewton knows more than do I."

"An inordinate amount, I am sure," agreed Miss Albury before Thea could speak. "The treasure hunt we are all so eager to conduct is for the future. But, in the meantime . . . curiosity is a most beguiling emotion, is it not, Miss Minturn?"

"And such a common one," murmured Mrs. Farraby, which made Thea choke and hope no one else had noticed the double entendre. She shot a reproachful glance at her cousin who met it blandly.

"The Long Gallery on the top floor, which holds the older portraits, is of the greatest interest," Mr. Tillingbourne began, "but we will start here with the library," and led the way.

"And none of these panels hold any secret?" asked Mr. Albury, tapping one with a small knife he whipped from his pocket. He was a stalwart youth in his late teens, so Thea judged.

"Any secret here behind panels would have been found by now," Lord Deveron said shortly. "And any panel that had been pried up would show the scars. You said this portion goes back to the time of Elizabeth, Mr. Tillingbourne?"

"That is certain. This wing was built by Sir Richard's father, then enlarged and redecorated by Sir Richard. He brought in Italian plasterers and painters to do the panels, some ceilings and fireplaces in the state rooms, for that was the period when the popularity of their plaster work began though it became more delicate and fanciful in later years." The saloons and dining room were politely admired and quickly left. "The bedrooms are on the first floor," Mr. Tillingbourne told them as he led them to some stairs. "They would hardly be of interest at the moment so we will continue to the second floor and the Long Gallery." The authoritative note of the guide rang through his words, and all followed him obediently. "There are two staircases that go from the hall to those above in addition to the one from the gatehouse which is seldom used. Here is the nearest."

The Long Gallery stretched along the front of the house and must once have been a ballroom. The mullioned windows and ancient panelling made it dark, though a footman was hurriedly lighting candles in the wall sconces. Four massive armchairs stood against the inner wall below a line of portraits in black frames. Miss Albury sent her glance along them. "It is a pity old portraits are so poorly done and dark that they can hold little appeal. But there are three, more recent I believe, quite good, in the large saloon in Deveron's mansion."

"If you are referring to the Van Dyck, the Romney, and the Gainsborough, they are much admired," Mr. Tillingbourne agreed politely. "Here," he led the way to the nearer of the two end fireplaces, "is one of special interest. You all know the story of the Zamora emeralds.

This lady above the mantel is Isabella Maria to whom they once belonged."

In the half-length portrait, whose painting was a little stiff, Isabella Maria was a girl in a dark red dress, with black curls and large eyes in a narrow haughty face. "It was painted at the order of Sir Richard while she—and he—awaited the ransom. It was believed that he was in love with her and that she repulsed him."

"But . . ." exclaimed Thea, "there . . . around her neck, wrists . . ."

"Precisely." Mr. Tillingbourne nodded approval. "Sir Richard was so infuriated by her escape that, with his own hand, either from grief or anger, he painted those black blobs you see where once the emeralds had shone. Apparently he enjoyed watching the Italian decorators as they moulded and painted the plaster decorations. It was said he did a frieze of ships for the fireplace in his bedroom but was dissatisfied with it and destroyed it."

Miss Albury's lip curled. "He should have held his hand here. That black quite spoils what might have been an amusing old picture. But then," her head moved and again her gaze swept down the line of portraits, "there is not much of interest here."

"Perhaps only for the family," suggested Mrs. Farraby gently.

"Sir Richard's wife—she was Lucy Freane—must have led an unhappy life," Mr. Tillingbourne continued as if nothing had been said. "She was married to him at sixteen, some months after the escape of his captive. That is her portrait on the other side of this door."

The group revolved to face a girl in brocade as white as her long wistful face. The eyes were light blue, and the pale gold hair stood out almost like a cloud behind her head. Between her hands lay a red rosebud. The sadness of her expression and the drooping lips were apparent in spite of the awkwardness of the painting.

"She bore Sir Richard two daughters, to his annoyance, and then a son who lived though she did not. There is no portrait of Sir Richard," Mr. Tillingbourne finished.

"When we search for the treasure we'll go over it all. We must do it quickly." Mr. Albury's enthusiasm for the project was very evident. He reached out and knocked on the nearest panel, and Mr. Tillingbourne frowned.

"It will be as Miss Minturn wishes," the lawyer told him repressively, "though, of course, Lord Deveron has a special interest."

"Has it ever been suggested," Thea asked pleasantly, damping down her irritation at the assumption her home could be searched at will, "that some descendant of Sir Richard might have found the emeralds and taken them into the other house and concealed them there? Or carried them unwittingly if they were hidden in some ornament?" The startled expressions were reward for her forbearance.

"It is possible. But," Mr. Tillingbourne shook his head, "it is unlikely, for if they had been found, it would have somehow been revealed. And I should probably warn you that since their story has been recounted in the London papers, on the occasion of the demise of his late lordship, the public has been reminded that they are still presumably in the house. I venture to suggest that if any untoward noise is heard, it is presumed to be a rat in the panelling and not a burglar, and no one attempt to discover the source."

"How amusing." Mrs. Farraby gave a light laugh. "You are advising us to lie in bed and quake while unknown men prowl the house?"

"No, no," Mr. Gifford said hastily. "No need for concern. Thieves wouldn't have enough time for a real search."

"My thought," approved Mr. Tillingbourne, "but I felt the warning should be given. Shall we descend."

Once again in the gatehouse Miss Albury thanked Thea graciously for a diverting hour and led the men across to the opposite hallway. Mr. Tillingbourne expressed warm appreciation of the day and luncheon and departed in his chaise.

"She is indeed a beauty," Mrs. Farraby allowed thoughtfully, watching the pink dress vanish. "Her features and coloring and figure are perfect."

"Her eyes are too small." Thea was happy to say it out loud. "She is in her Third Season."

"Then she will probably take Deveron, and he will be monstrously flattered." Mrs. Farraby shook her head. "But perhaps he will be a match for her later, though I doubt it." She touched Thea's arm. "After this strenuous day, my love, we would both do well to rest awhile before tea."

As she lay on her own bed that night, Thea found her thoughts centered on the blonde. Beautiful, yes, in her statuesque way, but was that all a man desired in a wife? Cordelia Albury was not endowed with more than adequate intellect or sensitivity, she was convinced, and not the wife for Lord Deveron. But it was evident she was regarding him favorably. She was fairly itching to get her hands on redecorating his house, and anything she did to it would be disastrous. Furthermore, she was curious beyond bounds. And the very air with which she strolled across the hall of the gatehouse was an offense.

Thea sat up. That was not permissible. Something must be done. She looked out the window to the line of hills and trees, dark in the moonlight, had her answer and giggled, something no lady was permitted unless alone. After two years in decorous check, her spirits were improving. She must remember not to give them free rein and not speak forthrightly as her parents had laughingly encouraged. But, at times, she would find ways to be herself. Tomorrow would be one.

Three

THE HEAVY DEW made a sheen on the grass as Thea, before breakfast, walked through the central courtyard toward the yew hedge, the stables, and the cottage of Mr. Wymond, the estate manager. A startled but sympathetic Brewton, discovered in the pantry, had advised consulting him and enlisting his aid, for he would bring in Hearne, the head of the stables, who could supply all that was needed. The dew was already losing its frostlike look as she went back to the house. She wished she were young and could run through it barefoot and make dark tracks and feel the cool wetness, but told herself she must put away such childish thoughts. Besides, she was hungry, and cook always furnished breakfast of a variety to tempt any taste. It was gratifying that Mr. Wymond had been understanding and approving and promised all assistance immediately.

Since Brewton took care of them himself at breakfast, Thea felt quite free to tell her Cousin Susan of her project. That lady laughed so hard she was unable to take any coffee for several moments and, on catching the gleam in Brewton's eyes and Thea's anticipatory glee, went off again. "I am going in search of some flowers, Thea, but I promise you I will not be long and will join you happily."

A crashing sound came faintly down the corridor. "It is nothing, ma'am," soothed Brewton as Mrs. Farraby jumped. "Merely some planks being deposited rather quickly."

"I must go and cut the flowers before the sun is too high." She finished her coffee and hurried away, as Thea and Brewton smiled.

Not until she heard the sound of hammering for several minutes did Thea wander down the stairs to the hall of the gatehouse where she surveyed with pleasure the activity of four men in white shirts and pantaloons. None of them could she recognize, but she presumed they came from the stables. They seemed perfectly competent so she sat down to watch. The sound of hammering echoing most satisfactorily around the stone wall must penetrate to the other morning room, or dining room, and eventually arouse curiosity.

Her wait was slightly longer than expected for the gentlemen apparently slept late. When she heard voices in the opposite hall, she rose and went down to the floor and placed herself in profile as if watching the activity, quite forgetting her hair was somewhat disheveled and the bottom of her green morning dress still damp.

"I'll stop that infernal din," Lord Deveron was saying loudly above Mr. Gifford's somewhat anxious, "Don't fly into the ropes, old boy, won't do any good," as the two men erupted into the hall and stopped.

"What the devil are you doing, ma'am?" Deveron exploded.

Looking surprised at seeing him, Thea sauntered in his direction. "Merely building a wall, my lord. It is going up in a most expert fashion. It is planned for only seven feet in height." She turned and surveyed the line of planks already nailed to uprights and the supports in place. "We are using old oak planks, you see, to be in keeping with the hall itself."

"And what is your notion, ma'am?" he asked with cold anger.

Thea twinkled at him. "Why, for our mutual protection, sir. It will insure that neither of us is disturbed by casual intruders from the other house." The memory of the casual intrusion of the afternoon before hung in the air between them. "With this in place it will be necessary to come to the entrance door of each house and inquire if a visit is convenient or, better still," she paused thoughtfully, "send a note before hand, as is proper."

"There is no need for this barrier," Deveron grated.

"But we will each feel so much more private when people are unable to stroll from one open hall to another."

His hand half rose and she knew he would have liked to slap her, but it dropped. The hammering had ceased, and the four men were carefully measuring some planks. "The wall is disfiguring," he said with an evident effort at control.

"But no one will see it, and if guests come they will enter the house they seek by the proper door. It will discommode no one since the stairs are independent, and the door at the back is wide and permits entrance to either side of the wall." She was so enjoying being reasonable she almost forgot her original annoyance. "All the construction is on my side, as you will see from the center chalk line at your feet."

"You should have consulted me."

He was even more handsome in his anger. Delighted at her success, Thea found herself laughing and realized happily that would infuriate him still further. "You must lower your pretensions, my lord," she gurgled. "We can each do as we wish in our own house. You have not asked if I approve of the new decorations planned for your rooms. Further, Mr. Wymond has approved of the wall." That, she felt, was a clincher.

"She has you there, Dev." Mr. Gifford left off his appraisal of the carpentry. "Good job they're doing. Gives privacy, you know."

"Quite my sentiments, Mr. Gifford." Mrs. Farraby wandered in through the door in front, a flat basket of daffodils on one arm.

Lord Deveron apparently had not heard them. "Miss Minturn, you should be guided by me as one more conversant with the polite world and its customs. That wall is unseemly, unnecessary and childish, but it should have been no surprise to me." With a glance that swept disdainfully over both Thea and the wall, he turned around and retreated. Mr. Gifford's, "Come down off your high horse, old boy," faded down the opposite hall. The hammering started so quickly the men might have been poised and waiting, as was Thea's laughter.

Exhilarated by the encounter, Thea waited for the next plank to be placed and went off with her cousin to the housekeeper's room to make friends with a chuckling Mrs. Brewton, who introduced cook. There followed a discussion of dishes that would be most favored by the ladies. The afternoon was spent going through some of the rooms, but not the attics or cellars, and tea was followed by a stroll down the drive to the lodge. They came in by the front door and admired the sturdy wall. At dinner Thea asked Brewton to extend her thanks to Mr. Wymond, Hearne, and the four workmen.

Perhaps it was the strong moonlight coming through the windows or the memories of rooms that chased each other through her mind, but Thea found her sleep broken. Once she thought she heard a squeak, but told herself no rat would dare show itself at Ardsley Hall. The thought was comforting and she had almost dropped off when she was sure she heard a scraping sound over her head. That was the Long Gallery, and there was no reason anything should scrape on those boards. Nothing up there was worth stealing. Another soft scrape dragged over her head.

Indignantly she got out of bed and into dressing gown and slippers. No one had any right in her picture gallery. At her door she recalled Mr. Tillingbourne's advice to let any burglar rob in peace, but there could be no burglar among those ancient portraits unless he had a clue to the emeralds and, if they were his goal, it was her duty to thwart him. She left open the door of her room for light to the stairs. There would be moonlight in the Long Gallery.

Two oblongs of brightness from the open doors lay across the upper hall. She edged to the nearest, hesitated, and peered around the door jamb. One of the heavy chairs was in front of the fireplace and on it stood a man, his hand raised to touch the portrait of Isabella Maria, not only touch but to feel, for his fingers were following the black line of blobs that covered the painted necklace. Only her coheir could have the effrontery to come so at night to examine that picture. It was the chair she had heard scraping. And she had him at a disadvantage for it was standing unevenly on the edge of the hearthstone.

Dressing gown and slippers did not conduce to a feeling of dignity, but at least her approach was silent as she walked into the gallery. "There was no need, Lord Deveron, for you to come like a thief in the night to examine that picture. I would have permitted you, of course, to carry out your search."

His back to her, he was a dark silhouette. The hand, long and white in the glow from the windows, lifted, the figure half turned on the chair seat, the chair overbalanced and crashed on its side throwing the man to the floor. To

Thea the sound seemed appalling, but there was only Cousin Susan to hear for the servants' rooms were too far away. What should she do if the man was injured? Leave him to get out by himself, she decided and backed away. But her curiosity rose and she found herself tiptoeing forward and bending down to peer at the face.

The figure stirred. "Very properly, Miss Minturn, I am at your feet," said a voice that held laughter.

"I trust no bones are broken to keep you there," she snapped. "I do not care for men lying at my feet at any time."

"No? I thought that the posture all young ladies preferred. However, if you insist . . . Come around in front and give me your hand, and I'll find out how the bones are working."

Not to be ordered about, she tiptoed to the door and listened to the quiet of the house, came back and circled the still recumbent figure, and held out her hand. It was grasped firmly and held a moment. "Head swimming a bit," the man muttered, "but no matter." He drew up his legs and half rose, the other hand groping for the side of the chair, and came to his feet, facing the windows, his eyes closed.

"You are *not* Deveron," she accused him and pulled at her hand.

He continued to hold it. "Steady me a minute," he muttered. Then, more strongly, "Would you rather I were?"

"Of course not," she said crossly. The moonlight made dark his hair and suddenly opened eyes and the hollows beneath the cheek bones. He didn't quite sway but there was a tremor in his hand, and she let him hold hers to save him from another crash to the floor.

"Uncommonly hard floors you have, Miss Minturn," he complained.

"Oak is apt to be hard and you came down from a

height," she pointed out. "What are you doing here and who are you?" If he could talk he could answer that.

The eyes closed and opened. "Had an idea," he explained, "when I read about Stanford's death. Remembered that paint on the picture, blobby and thick, and wondered if Sir Richard had put the emeralds underneath. He didn't." The tone was regretful. "Too obvious, I suppose. Besides, blobs are not big enough. Had a letter yesterday and had to find out quickly."

She peered at him more closely. "You're one of the men who helped build the wall this morning." she exclaimed.

He dropped her hand. "I wouldn't have been much good to Hadrian, but I offered to take the place of a groom needed elsewhere, and it got me inside."

The effrontery of the man! If he was going to search more, she couldn't stop him without rousing the house, and he wouldn't permit that. She must get him out. "Do you have any other ideas?" she asked coolly.

"Not at the moment." He began to shake his head and put up a hand to stop it.

"How did you get in?" She hoped it wasn't by a window.

"While helping on the wall you built to annoy Deveron, I slipped into the office and put back the lock on the door to the court."

"Then you had better go as you came. Now," she ordered.

"Yes, ma'am," he agreed meekly. "But you'll have to come with me in case I start to fall again."

She looked at his long length doubtfully, she couldn't sustain that frame if it began to totter. "You can hold on to the rail."

"I plan to. But I'll need you on the other side. Come on, like a good girl. It was you and your chair that made me fall." With some effort he set it upright, started to lift it, and stopped.

She ignored that. "But who are you?"

"Just a failed burglar and a neighbor. We can't talk here. Go and listen whether anyone is stirring."

There was no sound in the house as they moved slowly to the stairs and down to the ground floor. He held her arm firmly, and she could only presume he was also holding the balustrade. There was light enough in the office for him to move between desk and walls to a door she had not noticed. He opened it and looked back.

"You *are* a good girl. Any other would have gone into high hysterics. Meet me tomorrow, midmorning, at the bench where the river bends."

"What?"

"Oh, lord, forgot you don't know. Walk east from the yew garden, take the path down the ride—what looks like a lane but isn't—and when it forks take the right glade."

"Why should I come?" she asked indignantly.

"You've forgotten," and she was sure he was smiling, "but you're curious, you want to know who I am, and you're romantic. I'll tell you tomorrow morning. Now you better get to bed."

As she went up slowly, not because she had been so instructed but because she was sleepy, she began to be out of patience with herself. Her conduct this past half-hour had not been that of a properly brought up young female. She should have shrieked at discovering a strange man in the house and, when the servants arrived, have fainted gracefully. She should somehow have found out who he was and not made necessary this ridiculous tryst by the stream. Wistfully she wondered if enough noise could have been made to arouse Lord Deveron to come to her assistance, but decided that pleasing picture could not have been achieved owing to distance. Obviously it was her duty to discover who this burglar might be so as to guard against further invasions.

There seemed an air of anticipation, of something pleasant about to happen this morning, that was quite unaccountable. Thea dawdled over breakfast and found herself announcing casually she was going to take a little walk in the woods. Cousin Susan agreed absently that a walk was always excellent for the health at any time of day and was sure this one would be agreeable.

Thea let herself out the door of the office, crossed the court to the arch in the yew hedge, found a garden devoted to roses, wondered if there were knot and herb gardens but felt no inclination to discover them. Then she came on more yews that turned out to be another hedge around a space divided into triangular plots with four archways cut in the thick walls. One of them opened onto a lawn that melted into a wide alley between lines of oaks whose leaves were just uncurling. There could be no harm following this ride just for a distance to see where it led. She could turn back any time. There was a little resilience under foot that made walking a more agreeable exercise than the pavements of Bath. The air held a slight tang and trees and bushes showed charming variations in the green of new leaves. When the ride divided she followed the one to the right, and before she knew it there was a glint ahead, a line of cedars, a marble bench, and a figure rising as she approached.

"Why, I'm here," she exclaimed in surprise.

"Just where you intended all along," the man reassured her. "Your feet knew for you. Come sit down. I remembered this bench would not be clean and went to the trouble of bringing a cloth, so you must use it." He put out a hand. She put hers in it without thought and let him lead her to the bench and a strip of blue canvass that covered it.

"But I didn't mean . . ." she began with a touch of confusion.

"No, of course not," he soothed. "It is pleasant to find you more appealing in sunlight than in moonlight. The glimpse in the gloom of the gatehouse didn't count."

Since he was regarding her unashamedly, she looked back at him. His hair was dark brown, not black, and his gray eyes had flecks and without the shadows the hollow cheeks were less pronounced. In his left cheek was a thin scar which made a line beyond the corner of the firm mouth. "As you see, again," he began politely, "I am not as handsome as your Deveron."

"You're not," she nodded, "but he's not my Deveron. He's an abominable man."

"Bit highhanded, eh? Not surprising, when he's come into so much so soon and the army behind him. But you do ask for trouble."

"I don't. You don't understand." It would not be dignified to come to points with him. "I came, sir, to learn who you are."

Drooping willows bordered the stream but a patch had been cut away to reveal the bright water. The slow flow was soothing.

"I've been sitting here wondering if I should." He drew up one leg so his foot rested on the bench and clasped his arms around his knee. "Told myself if I was sensible I'd run away and not get involved, see some more of the world. But there's Deveron and the beauty, the confounded emeralds, Stanford's antic will, and you caught in its coil. A collection of questions, and to my surprise I find I'd like to watch for the answers. So here I am"— one hand waved—"enjoying the beauty of the riverbank."

If she had been standing, Thea would have stamped her foot. "You're babbling, and enjoying the sound of your own voice," she said coldly. "Either tell me who you are or get off my land."

He sighed. "Sad how the acquiring of property has an unfortunate effect. Very well, Miss Minturn, since you are so curious and determined, I will tell you I am a neighbor, recently home from distant lands. Also I am in some very distant degree a cousin, further removed than Deveron, you may be sure. My name is Laurent Brainerd, my title is Lord Bourne, and it's older than Deveron's and I've had it longer. I live at High Wyfells a mile or so across the stream and through the woods. I shall call you and Deveron cousin, if it pleases me."

"That makes no matter since it is known we cannot choose our relatives." She looked at him again. He was thin, perhaps he was being truthful about it all. "Are you the cousin who will follow Deveron by the will?"

"Certainly not. Stanford wouldn't play such a shabby trick on me. He liked me; I amused him, in spite of his scolds when I got into scrapes. I was sent down from Oxford and mightily enjoyed the life of a larky, day-go-mad lad in London, won a curricle race and lost horse and curricle at cards, liked Society, high and low, was caught in Dun Street and ordered out of the country in disgrace, after my father paid my bills. So I sailed off to find new excitements, and did, and ended up, to my surprise, in the army. I was the black sheep of all the families with which I was connected. Word came home I was dead; that made all the relatives like me since I was out of the way. Then I discomposed them by returning home, but since I brought a modest fortune all may now be forgiven."

She had been watching the amusement in the gray eyes. "I don't believe that fall last night made you dizzy at all. You were play-acting. You were really quite in control of yourself."

"You half wrong me, Miss Minturn. I could think of no other way to keep you there. And I was curious."

"So you reverted to your black sheep days and came to steal the emeralds?"

"How suspicious you are. Of course I wouldn't have

stolen them. As I said, a long-delayed letter came two days ago. If I could find those stupid emeralds, some friends would be saved a voyage and a deal of trouble avoided. I promise you there are no stones under that black paint."

"Falling off that chair served you right. But," she gave a sudden smile, "I must thank you for the effort you have saved me. I had the same thought and would have tried myself."

"So you're impulsive and curious and forthright and young and inexperienced. I'll wager you've had a patch of rough going in recent years, too, and the school mistressing—is my guess right?—was not very pleasant." He leaned along the bench and touched her cheek with one finger. "Poor child. There's rough going ahead for you, too."

His voice was so warm, his expression so kind, Thea felt tears at the back of her eyes. "I've guessed that," she whispered, and instantly told herself not to act like a ninny at unexpected sympathy and put up her head. "My father always said one goes lightly over bad ground. I'll come about."

"You will, if you do as I instruct you." He nodded and rose. "Stand up." His voice was now peremptory.

From recent habit she obeyed an order and then, appalled at herself, sat down and watched him as he backed away from the bench and looked her over. "Met any of the locals yet?" he asked curtly.

"Only Miss Albury and her brother."

"So she's preparing to settle for Deveron? Wise of her. Well, let me tell you, you and your companion better go straight to London and get some gowns to meet the gentry in. You look like a waif from an orphan's home in that frock. I'll wager you haven't a gown that wouldn't make Cordelia feel sorry for you—if she can feel sorry for anyone but herself. Tell Tillingbourne. He'll make arrangements, see to the blunt you need, and pay the bills. You owe it to Stanford—he'd not be pleased to have his heir pitiable—and to yourself. Set about it right away, now."

She eyed him with growing hostility, his faded pantaloons and shirt and muddy boots. He said he had known Lord Stanford, but that didn't bestow on him the right to give her directions as to her conduct. "I suppose *you* can wear anything you want."

"Of course. I belong and you don't—yet. You'll never get that husband you need if you go around looking like a dowd, even down here. Don't forget the riding habit. Go to Lucille, she's the best, or was six years ago. She can put you on to the right shops besides her own. But don't mention my name. Last bit of fluff I took there didn't pay her bills with the money I gave her, and I didn't learn of that soon enough. Lucille will fix you up, fine as ninepence."

She nodded thoughtfully. "You are rude and shameless, you know, and excessively provoking because you are quite right." She would not have thought of clothes and London, she had to acknowledge. She jumped up. "I'll set about it. Won't you escort me to the house?"

"Why? To protect you from all those wild birds and wild flowers? You got here on your own, you'll make it safely to the Hall. Don't tell anyone but old Tillingbourne what you're about. Lie low in town. You don't want anyone to see you until you are ready."

"Again you are outrageous and right." She gave him a nod. "Thank you for your good advice," she said stiffly, for it did not come easily to admit even by indirection she had been so wanting in perceptions.

He surveyed her again—"Good luck"—gave her a little bow, and was gone down the path away from the bench.

Again she was annoyed at herself for not discovering more about this man and allowing him to tell her what to do, but had to admit she must be grateful to him.

Cousin Susan agreed instantly. "I did not like to suggest our wardrobes needed attention, love, for I was convinced you would come to that conclusion shortly. We go tomorrow? Splendid."

Four

TO THEA it was again a fairy tale she could not quite believe as she sat in the tasteful white and rose salon of Lucille while gowns of every type were brought out for her inspection. Delicately Lucille had endeavored to discover how Miss Minturn had learned of her establishment, but Thea had only mentioned that Ardsley Hall was near the village of Tewin which, in turn, was not far from the town, Dylson, where Mr. Tillingbourne, to whom the bills would be sent, resided.

"Tewin," the stately modiste had murmured. "Yes. . . . Once there was a gentleman, a most charming, laughing young man of perfect address and a deplorable taste in, er, young ladies. I forget his name. Also the home of Miss Cordelia Albury is not far, as I recollect." Doubtless there had been a number of wild young men who lived in the vicinity of Tewin, Thea told herself, as she regarded a ballgown of pale green with a ethereal overskirt of pale blue gauze, and learned the direction of the best hair dresser who had sufficiency of taste not to be swept away by any mode of the moment.

To Thea's delight, Cousin Susan proved to be a different creature in London. In Ardsley she had maintained an aloof and calm reassurance, approving cheerfully of every proposal. In London she carried herself with the air of one who belonged, and her manner was distinguished but kind. She found the Stanford house very acceptable and in five minutes gently reduced the housekeeper to subservience. After dinner the first day, she went with new briskness to the desk in the small saloon, which was done in a pleasing pale yellow, announcing, "We must make lists you know, my love, for without lists one is lost. We must find some recent numbers of *Mirror of Fashion,* perhaps at Hookhams, and discover what are the latest modes, for though Lucille is doubtless up on everything we must form our own judgments. What a pity we cannot attend a rout or even the opera." She paused and gave Thea a slow smile. "And friends, also, I must list a few, but you are right, we cannot be seen until we are ourselves refurbished." She was as assured as a general preparing to manage an army.

"I need a new riding habit," put in Thea as though the words had been spoken in her ear.

"Of course. So let us prepare for tomorrow."

That afternoon, after two cups of tea, Cousin Susan set her cup down firmly. "My dear Thea. I have given a matter some thought and am now convinced I should follow the lines of my duty and speak out. May I?"

"Of course, ma'am," Thea agreed, a trifle apprehensively.

The gray curls nodded. "You are a sensible girl. But you have not had advantages so necessary for you to encounter with success the circles into which you will be moving. Do you waltz?"

Sadly Thea shook her head.

"So I feared. I will find an instructor for you, for it is of the first importance that one be featherlight in the waltz and at ease in the figures of the quadrille, the boulanger, and the country dances. Of course, you cannot waltz until you are given permission by one of the patronesses of Almack's, and we will need vouchers, but I am making plans. You have never had the opportunity of serving tea in your own home to guests, or curtseying to a duchess, or entering a room full of curious people, or even descending a long stair in a ball gown. These things do not change, and I can show you. You are wondering how? After all, my dear child, I am the granddaughter of a duke—a slightly impoverished one it is true—but we did visit and entertain, and I did have a Season. It is my intention to see that you acquire all the social graces you may need so you will do us credit and be at ease yourself. And do not concern yourself that you may be a touch reserved in your manner, for that will please the dowagers, and they will consider you a pretty-behaved girl, which is a useful accolade, I assure you."

Thea pulled her chair over to the table. "Dear ma'am, you are so kind. I have known there is much of which I am ignorant and was quite at a standstill when I tried to consider how I might learn. I will be grateful for all you can do, for I know it is what my parents and Lord Stanford would wish."

Cousin Susan patted her arm. "Of course, dear child, and since you are graceful and know much already, we will contrive very well."

The next afternoon upon returning from shopping for evening bags and gloves to match two of her new gowns, accompanied by Cadwell, the experienced, middle-aged abigail who had been found by the housekeeper and approved by Cousin Susan, Thea discovered there was company for tea. A spare, gray-haired man was listening with absorbed amusement to her cousin describing life in Dorset.

"Thea, my love," she beamed. "Permit me to present an old friend, Lord Ledgefield. Just fancy, it is quite fifteen years since we have met, and we find we entertain each other as famously now as we did then. Ralph, this is my cousin, Miss Minturn, of Ardsley Hall."

The gentleman, clad in correct dark jacket and pale pantaloons, made a bow of a precision that came from military life, Thea was sure, as she made a little curtsey.

"It was to Sidonie, Lady Ledgefield, you understand, one of my oldest and dearest friends, that I sent a note of our arrival, and Ralph came himself to tell me he had lost her five years ago. So sad, and a great disappointment for I had counted on her assistance. But tomorrow he will bring a friend, a Mrs. Kent, who has made a name for herself in instructing new arrivals in town who are desirous of entering Society. There are undoubtedly some changes in customs these past years of which I could not be aware, and Mrs. Kent will provide both knowledge and a distinguished polish."

"Which you ladies would hardly need," Lord Ledgefield interjected gallantly, "but I understand your situation, and you will find her a most amiable and helpful person."

What with the sessions and expeditions with Mrs. Kent, the dancing lessons and the fittings, the seven-day visit extended to nearly three weeks, all most frivolous and utterly delightful. When the new clothes arrived—and since the Season had not really commenced—Cousin Susan felt they could enjoy some discreet outings with Lord Ledgefield such as a concert and an afternoon stroll in Hyde Park. When they returned at last to Ardsley Hall, a hired coach followed them with their boxes and Cadwell.

"Welcome home, Miss Minturn," Brewton beamed at the bottom of the steps to the gatehouse.

"That's the first time I have been so welcomed in over two years." Thea's smile was surprised and glowing. "Thank you, Brewton. Pray come and tell us what has occurred; I cannot wait to hear." She was untieing the ribbons of her bonnet and cloak as she went in the door, nodded approvingly at her wall, and entered the library.

Brewton appeared with a silver salver of cards. "There have been callers, Miss Minturn, as might be expected," he began.

"Please tell me. The names won't mean a thing to me." She went to the window to be sure the sweep of lawn to the trees and the layers of hills were as lovely as she remembered.

"Very well, miss. There was Lady Albury and Miss Albury, and surprised, if I might say so, not to find you in residence."

"How nice," said Thea delightedly. "Come, Cousin Susan, and listen to our callers."

"Squire and Mrs. Chilworth, they live to the south," continued Brewton, turning over the cards. "Lord Haslam, a good friend of Lord Stanford. Mrs. Bendish and her oldest son. Mr. Gifford twice. The Misses Halsey of Rose Cottage in the village."

"The village tabbies, no doubt," smiled Thea. "Is that all?"

"There were a few others, ma'am, but they can wait. There was also what I might call a visitation. I did not care for it, but under the circumstances I could see nothing I could do to prevent it."

Thea began to bristle. "A visitation? Surely not of spirits." She almost knew already.

"Of very solid persons, miss. It was six days ago, in the afternoon, when Lord Deveron, Miss Albury, Mr. Gifford, and Mr. Albury came to the front door. Lord Deveron inquired if you were home and seemed a little put out that you had not returned. Though, if I might say so, I am sure they were all well aware of that. He then told me they wished to search the house for the emeralds.

"I said you would doubtless return in a few days and

be pleased then to accompany then. But Miss Albury pointed out they might as well go around now and spare you that trouble, and Mr. Albury added that Lord Deveron had every right to search and that you would also benefit from any discovery they might make. I thought his lordship a little hesitant, but Miss Albury walked in, and there was no way I could prevent her. But when I saw Mr. Albury carried a hammer and only caught his arm in time to prevent him from tapping on the ornament there on the panel beside the fireplace I stayed with them the entire time."

"You were quite right, of course, Brewton, and thank you. Did he try any more tapping?" Thea asked with interest.

"He was about to tap the panels in the saloon when again I stopped him, pointing out that plaster, wood, and even stone, can be damaged by blows. When he insisted it was necessary to find if any panels were hollow I sent for a stick of wood for him to use, since that would not be likely to dent oak but which did bring forth a sufficiency of sound to satisfy him, and prevented his attacking anything else."

"But where did they go?" Her sense of outrage was mounting.

"Through all the rooms on the two lower floors, miss, and the gallery. Fatigue, I believe, dissuaded Miss Albury from the attics and cellars."

"And even in my bedroom?" She must remain calm, she knew.

"I tried to point out it was a gross impropriety, miss, but they would not hear since it is the State bedroom and once Sir Richard's. I can assure you nothing was found."

"You behaved most admirably, Brewton, and it must have been excessively awkward for you. Thank you. I see there is something I must do." She snatched up her cloak and sped out to the door, around to the other door, and tugged strongly at the bell rope. Since it was late in the afternoon, the men might well be in for tea. She was about to pull again when a heavy-set butler opened the door.

"Good afternoon. Kindly announce to Lord Deveron that Miss Minturn is calling and would appreciate the favor of a few words," she told him crisply and followed him into the hall of the house and up wide stairs to the first floor, not giving him the opportunity, if it had come to his mind, of indicating the attending room or some spot for her to wait. They passed through a long white and gold saloon and into a smaller room with panels decorated in a pleasing blue that matched the rug. Thea paused at the door to give the butler a moment to announce her and then, dropping her cloak on a chair on the way, advanced toward the tea table by the window where the two men were lounging.

They rose, their faces expressing surprise and a little shock, and bowed. Lord Deveron managed "Miss Minturn, a pleasure . . ."

She allowed him no more. "Since it seems to be the thing to visit between these two houses informally," she began sweetly, noting she had not been asked to sit down, "I have come without ceremony to your home, my lord, as you did to mine."

Though he looked back steadily a faint flush rose on his cheeks. "I, and my friends, did call, Miss Minturn," he acknowledged. "To our regret, we found you absent."

"Which you knew from the other visits of your friends." She was pleased she was holding to a sweet, reasonable voice. "Do you not intend to offer me a chair, my lord? I am sure you were not so scurvily treated in my house even in my absence."

This time he visibly flushed and went quickly to bring an armchair near the table. Graciously she thanked him and seated herself and waited until they had also. "And whose idea was it to go through my house on an exhaustive search though I was away?" she asked.

"Mine, of course," he answered stiffly, and Thea had to give him points for being a gentleman and not blaming a lady. "The discovery of the emeralds would be of benefit to us all."

"And after waiting over two hundred years it was not felt that could be delayed by a few days, I understand. And one of your party had no compunction in attempting to knock off parts of the decorations or damage the panelling in the search," she continued. A gulping sound from Mr. Gifford encouraged her. "I have, you see, a devoted major-domo who was considerably agitated by what he held to be the gross impropriety of the whole situation." She stopped and eyed the tea table where little remained. "Perhaps someone should instruct you in the niceties of your new situation as a home owner, Lord Deveron. It is customary to offer refreshment to even the most unwelcome guest."

From his glare it was apparent he would like to strangle her.

"But, as I might have expected, some of your staff are conversant with polite custom." Out of the corner of her eyes she had seen the butler bearing a silver tray with teapot, cups, and cakes, advancing through the doorway. There was silence while he placed all on the table and removed the used cups and plates and withdrew. Lord Deveron was sitting straight in his chair, one hand clenched around his napkin, awaiting the chance to speak. That must not be allowed, for she had learned that with miscreants of any kind it is a mistake to permit them to put into words what they conceive to be their justifications for wrong doing.

"Furthermore," she went on swiftly, "you and your party, with complete lack of sensitivity or nicety of mind, had the insolence to invade my bedroom and search that in every manner possible."

"Not that," muttered Mr. Gifford.

"Yes," she contradicted, "and I hope Miss Albury enjoyed the examination of my possessions along with you."

"Coming too strong, ma'am," Mr. Gifford said distinctly. "Gentlemen waited in the hall."

"So she deemed it her duty to search my things herself, and it was naturally necessary to go through chest and wardrobe looking for a secret drawer. I must assure you, my lord, if I were to search this house, I would not consider entering your bedroom or allowing any friend to do so, for we do like our privacy, do we not?"

Unfortunately, she saw, she had given him time to master his rage and the outburst to which she had looked forward was now smothered. He placed the napkin he had been crushing on the table and leaned back, his brows still drawn in a frown but his flush fading. "You are quite right, Miss Minturn," he began in a voice now chill and distant. "I admit I took a unpardonable liberty. However, I hardly feel that you have the—shall we say, experience —to be in a position to instruct me as to my conduct. You must be charitable—the enthusiasm of our discussion— your house at hand—the opportunity—you must forgive our eagerness."

"In spite of your pretensions, sir, it is not for you to tell me what I must and must not do." Indignation was at last making her lose the note of sweetness she had held so long. "If appealed to, enthusiasm I might understand. But such shocking want of conduct as to insist, over Brewton's protests, that strangers roam through a private home without permission, I cannot find it in me to forgive." She looked at the tea table and realized she was hungry. She rose. "Since you do not seem able to learn from your butler, I will thank you for the tea you did not offer me—fortunately—for I would have been compelled to refuse to break bread with you." She nodded toward them. "Good day, gentlemen," and swept across the room, hoping it looked as if she were sweeping, picking up her cloak on the way.

She was at the door when she heard Mr. Gifford say, "Might have known she has spirit. Looks quite different when she's on her high horse. Looks different from last time, too." Only a determined effort of will propelled her through the door and out of hearing of Lord Deveron's reply.

She thoroughly enjoyed recounting the incident, over tea, to Cousin Susan who went into a spell of laughter. Thea, conscious that Brewton was lingering in the hall, hoped he was enjoying what he heard.

"I do think you went somewhat beyond the bounds of judicious indignation, my love," Cousin Susan managed at the end.

"I think so now myself," Thea admitted. "And he was a gentleman about taking the blame. But then I see that . . . that *creature* . . . prying in my room . . . the very thought is shocking. What a relief that I had taken practically everything I owned with me."

"True, love, but pray forget it all, for I believe you will find among your letters one informing us of a small affair at Casons. Brewton has been telling me word of the plans is known."

A properly formal note it was, from Lady Albury inviting them to a small dance and supper, and the date only two days away.

"It would have been distressing to have missed it," Cousin Susan pointed out, "for this will be undoubtedly an opportunity to look over some of the eligible gentlemen of the countryside. The Albury affairs must be popular, and with the thought of the attendance of both Lord Stanford's heirs no one will remain at home. We have heard Lord Stanford spread the terms of his will far and wide, which seems to me deplorable, but apparently he was proud of it."

"Yes, and he gave no thought to the embarrassing position in which we are placed. If I allow my mind to dwell on it, I will be cast into the depths and never able to believe I have any attractions of my own."

"Never feel that way, Thea, for it is not true. And I must say the wisest course would be to ignore what occurred here."

"I will, ma'am, though I do regret it will not be difficult, for I have never been able to hold anger, or even a grudge, for more than a very short while. . . . What shall we wear?"

"Not our best, of course, for that would be in the worst taste, but not so simple we might seem to be disdaining the county society. Our boxes will be unpacked by now. Let us confer."

Thea regretted that she must wear white, or a pale shade, and that she could not waltz, for she had found herself adept and developed a decided partiality for the dance, but even here to waltz would label her as fast, and some word would inevitably be carried back to one of the patronesses in London and jeopardize the receiving of the so necessary vouchers to Almack's. She also regretted that when she took a casual morning stroll the next day to the stream, she enjoyed its beauties alone, though she told herself that was the proper way to appreciate Nature. But she found herself wondering if Lord Bourne, who had claimed to be a neighbor, would appear at the small dance.

Five

THE TIMING of their arrival had been judged to a nicety, for the Ardsley coach entered the string approaching Casons so that it was neatly in the center of the arrivals. In spite of an admonition from Cousin Susan not to allow her face to be seen at the window, as it would be taken as an evidence of vulgar curiosity, Thea could not refrain from peering. The house was a gray rectangle, with a clocktower supported by fat white pillars jutting out in the front, and a wing with long windows above a terrace and balustrade. She sat back quickly, suddenly overcome, she admitted, by the thought she would know no one in the place and would doubtless spend the evening sitting beside her cousin.

"Fear not, my child." The warm voice was comforting. "All will be most anxious to meet the heiress who has dropped in their midst. You will be quite the rage, but of course you will show no consciousness of that. If Lord Deveron should beg the privilege of a dance, for he will put it that way even if he does not mean it, I beg you will accord him your hand with the utmost graciousness, for it would not do for any word of a rift at Ardsley to reach the gossips."

It appeared that half the county was already in the ball room when Thea followed Mrs. Farraby to the receiving line. Lady Albury, slightly larger than her daughter, was coolly cordial. Cordelia showed not a trace of embarrassment as she greeted the two. Perhaps she has no idea I have heard of her conduct, Thea thought, and gave a wider smile than she had intended. Sir William was redfaced and round and hearty in his welcome. Young Mr. Albury appeared, begged the favor of the first dance as his right, and vanished.

Thea and her cousin were standing near a window, attempting to look as though they could see nothing nor be seen by any one, and conversing about nothing when a deep voice surged toward them. "Susan! You have not changed. No one told me it was you who had accompanied Stanford's heiress." An imposing figure in purple satin advanced on Mrs. Farraby.

Quite as tall and stately but considerably more spare, she moved forward to the encounter, her lavender silk the only color that could blend with the purple. "And indeed I had no idea you lived here, dear Erica, but if I saw a purple dress in the Sahara I would know you still could not resist your deplorable affection for that violent shade."

"Like it," said the deep voice, "and you, I see, have not outgrown the regrettable influence of your mother which kept you so long in sad pallids." Thea watched with fascination as the two heads of puffs and curls, one gray, one improbably black, met so delicately the cheeks never quite touched. "And this is Stanford's little cousin," said the voice. "Ummm . . . different, better than I expected. I never stand on ceremony, my dear. Permit me, however, to introduce my rapscallion nephew who has kept quiet for a longer period than is customary. Mrs.

Farraby, Miss Minturn, Lord Bourne."

"You must stop calling me rapscallion, dear aunt, for you will give the ladies quite an erroneous idea of my essentially serious and helpful nature." The voice held the laugh it had hinted before. Thea shifted one foot and faced a long lean figure in a midnight blue superfine coat and white breeches. The gray eyes glinted at her before he bowed over Mrs. Farraby's hand. "Your servant, ma'am," he said with a flourish and, glancing at Thea before executing his bow, "of course, yours also, Miss Minturn."

"Don't believe him, he's no one's. Silly convention. But you might give me a name, sir."

"When you permit me, ma'am. Ladies, my most delightful aunt, Lady Erica Hadham."

"Considering the other aunts, that ain't saying much," she sniffed, "but at least it's done. Susan, you and I must have a coze. You young things go and dance," and she waved a black chicken-wing fan at them.

"Sound advice," began Lord Bourne, but Mr. Albury was bowing to Thea. "The first dance, Miss Minturn. You promised."

She could only agree and give a small smile as Bourne bowed slightly, and let herself be led toward where the set was forming.

"Had to ask you," Mr. Albury explained as they went, "though a pleasure, of course. My father gave me a terrific scold, quite rolled me up, for wanting to knock on the walls of your house to look for hollow places. Cordy told him—didn't need to—just like a sister, and she thought you wouldn't hear. *I* knew you would but I didn't say so, or she'd do something else mean." They were separated by the figure, which Mr. Albury followed with the energy of youth. He was round-faced and sturdy and cheerful like his father. "Father said I must apologize to you first thing," he went on when they came together again. "So I do. But . . ." They separated briefly, and he went on in a moment, "I'm not sorry for I don't think there's anything back of all those panels. But I hope you forgive me." Obviously relieved when Thea told him she did, he devoted himself to giving her tips on badger and rabbit hunting until the dance ended, and he returned her to the side of her cousin.

A pause gave Thea a chance to look over the ballroom, and for the first time she felt a faint pity for Lord Deveron. Because of Cordelia's age, it must have been Lady Albury who had taken so enthusiastically to the Egyptian style. The floor was black and white marble squares, and the walls white. Between the windows were rounded white pilasters resembling pillars, each mounting from a cluster of black lotus leaves to a crown of drooping black palm leaves just below the black and white dado. Panels at each end featured pyramids and sphinxes, outlined in black. White curtains, bordered by the Greek key pattern, descended at the windows. The chairs were rounded half circles supported by mysterious animals that might have been cats. At the far wall a black marble slab of a table was held up by four gold pillars resting on the backs of alligators snarling at each other. The effect was overwhelming, and obviously it would be only a step from Egypt to the Pompeian decor probably planned for Ardsley. She was glad that, when Lady Albury brought over a young man who had come from the next county just for the ball, there was no need to make any comment on the room.

The Albury family did their duty by their guest, constantly introducing young gentlemen so Thea was well partnered, even for the Lancers, which Lady Albury explained was a sad romp and permitted only in the informality of the country. Thea was content to sit that one out with an awkward man who could talk of nothing but the pleasures of country living. He and the Lancers finished together and, since the stamina of all seemed inexhaustible, the band was tuning again when a figure of quiet elegance was bowing before her.

"Miss Minturn," began Lord Deveron, "may I have the pleasure of this dance?" He spoke as pleasantly as though they had just been introduced.

It's not fair, she thought as she rose, for anyone to be so handsome and assured, from the dark locks in the Brutus cut to the toes of his dancing pumps, making every other man look a trifle disordered. Of course she would dance with him. She raised her hand to place it on the offered arm when it was caught.

"For shame, Deveron," said an amused voice. "You cannot be serious. This dance is most evidently a waltz, and Miss Minturn would be ruined socially if she should waltz with you even in the country, as you know."

Thea listened, heard the beat, and smiled up at Lord Bourne's thin face. "You are quite right, sir, and I thank you for rescuing me, for I had not noticed the music and might have been on the floor before I discovered its nature, and the ensuing scene would have been embarrassing for us both."

Once more the blue eyes were flashing daggers at her, but before he could recover from his slight discomfiture she added brightly, "Perhaps Lord Deveron does not believe those vouchers will be coming my way so it could not matter what I danced now, or perhaps he prefers I should make myself ineligible for them." She hoped her smile was forgiving and was very conscious her hand had been placed on a dark blue sleeve.

"That is an outrageous thing to say, Miss Minturn," Deveron began in a very controlled voice. "You are insulting. . . ."

"No, no, no insult intended, I am persuaded," soothed Lord Bourne. "Perhaps just a realistic recognition of possibilities. I will rescue you both and take Miss Minturn for a stroll on the terrace. But, for the sake of appearances," he added softly, "I hope your pleasure of a dance is only postponed."

"I do not need you to instruct me in my duty, Bourne."

"Of course not, just two old soldiers discussing tactics. What a pity pleasure apparently cannot, in this instance, combine for you with duty. For me, it is pure pleasure. This window, Miss Minturn, gives on the terrace. May I escort you?" Somehow Thea found herself going through the window to a terrace where huge urns alternated with torches in high cages.

"That was really quite shocking, dear Miss Minturn," said Bourne as he led her toward the shadow by an urn. "I almost blushed for you. No, no," as she snatched her hand from his arm. "I am not condemning. Doubtless you had provocation for your thoughts which you expressed so pungently. It's an awkward situation for you both, of course, but you really must strive for a little conduct and curb your tongue and not so freely express what comes to your mind."

"Will you stop being so obnoxiously correct and soothing?" she demanded furiously. "How I speak to Deveron is none of your business. You sound like . . . like a Solomon and a nanny."

"No! Do I really? A combination that would not have occurred to me, though I discern the point you are making. But peace between the two of you is essential for your near future and that I merely hoped to indicate." He backed away and looked her up and down as he had by the cedars. "You did very well in London. Your hair is right now and that cream-colored silk and net and blue ribbon in your hair are just right for you on this occasion."

"You do me too much honor, sir," Thea snapped, "but . . ."

He laughed. "Don't get on your high horse with me.

It is not grateful of you since you admit I am always right." He shifted and looked through the window. "When we return you will see that your cousin and my aunt are quite the belles, surrounded two deep, no less. Aunt Erica is known for her sharp tongue and kind heart, and your Mrs. Farraby is not only welcome as a new face but as a source, they hope, of information about the progress of the heirs."

"They don't know my cousin," Thea said proudly.

"No doubt she'll rout them, horse, foot, and dragoons, with Aunt Erica guarding the rear. But we have stayed here within the limits of propriety, and I will now return you to the ballroom and the hovering Mr. Gifford." Without ceremony he took her back to Gifford, and she could only regret their talk had been so brief, for he was evidently a man of experience and would be a source of all kinds of information, if she could get any out of him.

It was even more difficult to conduct any coherent conversation during a quadrille than during a country dance, but Mr. Gifford contrived to communicate his approval of her appearance—dash it all, you look different—and that evidently her turn in London had put her in top form. She had only the need to ask him if he enjoyed his days at Ardsley to set him into a somewhat garbled string of reminiscences, so she felt free to look over the assemblage. They were a pleasant-looking collection but not so fashionable as many seen at the Assemblies at Bath. Many appeared wedded to country life and dress, but there were a number of well-garbed gentlemen and ladies with a definite air of Society about them. The girls were pretty, but none could equal Cordelia. The men were more varied, but Thea saw none to attract her interest. However, it was not fair to judge people in such a superficial way, she was thinking, and to her surprise heard Gifford saying earnestly as they met ". . . know you'll do the right thing, Miss Minturn," and was relieved when they separated. What had the man been saying? As they joined to promenade, she asked forthrightly, "What would be what you consider the right thing about what?"

"Thought you weren't listening," he said calmly, as she contrived to look regretful. "Natural. Can't listen to everything. Just saying know you're kind. Know you'll get married even if it aint what you want. Selfish if you don't. Keep Devèron from getting his share of Ardsley and . . ."

If they had not been on the floor, she would have drawn away from him. "Why should I ruin my life for the convenience of Lord Deveron?" she asked dangerously. "He has done nothing but issue orders and behave in a manner rude beyond conceiving."

"Dev was upset," Mr. Gifford carried on at the next opportunity. "Not like him. Deuced agreeable, usually. Will be again now he's going to get the wife he wants. You wouldn't put a spoke in *that* wheel."

Since she could hardly say that would give her pleasure, she was glad the figure called for a stamp with one foot. "Why should I help him? Will she have him, do you think?"

"Might not have before. I'll lay money she will now."

That was carrying frankness too far, Thea thought, but the dance was closing. "I'll think on it," she tossed over her shoulder as they separated for the last time. But as they walked from the floor he was saying anxiously, "Not enough, Miss Minturn. Know you'll not be selfish."

"You are above yourself," she exploded but calmed in time as Lady Albury intercepted them, sent Mr. Gifford for lemonade, and drew Thea down on a small sofa.

"Dear Miss Minturn," she began, "We were so cast down, not finding you at home when we called. Now, of course, I am rushed to death for we remove to town in two weeks for the Season."

"Of course," Thea agreed. "It would be unconscionable to deprive Society of the company of the beautiful Miss Albury." As she said it she knew she meant it, for while she could not like the girl she was compelled to admire her statuesque loveliness, but realized her words were another example of speaking too quickly, as Bourne had warned her.

However, Lady Albury gave her a surprised glance and her manner warmed a trifle. "How kind of you. . . . Yes, we are looking forward to the gaieties in spite of the fatigues they bring. Have you plans of your own?" It was asked in a kindly fashion, and Thea was glad to disclaim any plans and saw her companion relax further. "Too soon, undoubtedly. How agreeable it will be for Lady Erica to have such a dear friend in residence so close at hand. There will be more occasions like this, you know, even though some of us transfer to our townhouses, and I am persuaded you will find much here to attract you in the coming months."

Before Thea could contemplate the implications of that remark, Mr. Gifford had brought the lemonade, which she thought too weak, and Lord Deveron was beside her and asking for the privilege of conducting her to the country dance now forming. She smiled at all and allowed him to escort her to the nearest incomplete set.

With regret, she knew she must apologize. So at the first encounter, eyes lowered, she said softly, "I was rude beyond excuse about the waltz, and I am sorry." When she raised her eyes she found him looking over her head.

"Of necessity, you are forgiven, and even Bourne," he said flatly. "We really must converse and appear pleased with each other," he added before they separated. "Pray endeavor to smile, or the company will be convinced we are at even more swords' points than we are."

As they met again she gave a little laugh and nodded. "You are quite right, my lord, and we can at least discuss our domestic arrangements, though I find that excessively dull."

His eyebrows rose. "I am surprised. I would have thought them your chief interest, since I gather your life has been limited." He held a pleasant expression that quite made her heart turn over in spite of his words, but there was neither warmth nor interest in his gaze. At the next opportunity he asked if she cared to discuss her experiences teaching and on being told firmly she did not, he glanced over the dance floor. "Since we have so little in common we are reduced to commenting on this country collection. Do you believe that languishing girl in the horrid shade of pink will ever receive an offer?"

After an opportunity to observe the girl during a figure Thea told him when next they met, "She will droop over some stalwart man and proclaim her need for a strong arm to protect her from the harsh world and thus bemuse him into an offer to provide that arm." She laughed at the picture in spite of herself.

There was a little surprise in his glance. "You may well be right. That red-haired squire's son, now, which girl will be the bride he will choose?"

On what Thea felt a rather low level, they continued to discuss the guests, Lord Deveron with all the disdain of a London man of the world, which annoyed her because of its condescension, though she found it amusing. It was not amusing when, as the dance ended, he said kindly, "I feel our observations have been accurate but you will undoubtedly find some people in the neighborhood who are congenial and will feel quite at home in this society after a short while. And, with due care, you and I may rub along tolerably well."

"But we had better keep at a distance," she said firmly. Though she seethed inwardly at his condescension she gave him a last smile.

Thea had hoped that Lord Bourne would take her to

supper, but a presentable young man was brought up by Cordelia for that purpose, and Thea could hardly refuse. Between parrying polite but persistent questions from her table companions and the dancing that followed, she was relieved when Cousin Susan ordered the coach.

"We have departed a little early," she conceded as she settled against the squabs, "but not beyond permission, and our tact at leaving them time to speculate about us will be appreciated. On the whole, it was an enjoyable evening, did you not think so? How agreeable it is to find dear Erica a neighbor. Her nephew seems a charming man. She tells me he has given over the wild ways of his youth, due, she believes, to increasing years and two wounds he received. He was in the army on that unfortunate expedition to some port in South America. I never did understand how that came about or why we failed. He had innumerable adventures and was reported killed. Since he was not, he turned to businesses of some sort and has returned with vast sums such as the Brainerds have never possessed. And I must say I thought you and Lord Deveron behaved admirably together, which I am sure made the right impression."

Thereupon she murmured something about fatigue and fell into a light doze, while Thea tried to find comfort in contemplating her own evening.

It was high time, Thea decided, over her solitary breakfast that she give some thought to her present, her near future, and the distant future. She would go and walk in the woods, different woods, for exercise and fresh air were said to clear the mind. She left the gardens behind and was starting across a rough lawn when a figure came purposefully toward her. His country garb of canvas pantaloons and cloth jacket matched her simple morning dress. Like her, he wore no hat, and was more attractive and somewhat more approachable than on the dance floor.

"Miss Minturn, good morning." Lord Deveron bowed a little. "I was leaving the stables when I saw you and I seize this opportunity. Will you walk with me a few minutes? Those woods ahead are neutral ground." His manner was polite so she agreed, but with a little reserve.

He fell into step beside her and remained silent until they were under the first oaks. There he stopped and leaned against a wide trunk. "Miss Minturn. On our return from Casons last night my friend Gifford gave me as severe a set-down as he is capable of about my want of conduct toward you. Never have I heard him in such a taking. I was forced by his upbraiding to look back over our encounters. As we both realize, and have been told too often, we are in an awkward situation. Last night you said we should maintain a distance between us. That seems to me sensible, in view of our disparate lives and interests. Your cousin is obviously a lady accustomed to the higher circles of Society and will be of assistance to you in view of the experience you lack, for a school is hardly the best preparation for entering Society, no matter how excellent a family may be yours."

He was trying to be kind and reasonable, and Thea decided to let him have his say.

"But we will be forced to deal with each other from time to time, and while we shall keep the distance we desire, it will still be possible to deal properly. I am aware that the situation is as much abhorred by you as by me, and that at times my conduct has not been conciliatory. I hereby offer my apologies for what I may have said or done that has been offensive to you." The stiffness of his stance and words showed that this was not easy for him.

She would have liked to give him a set-down herself and recount all his misdeeds. But he was right in saying they might have to meet on various matters, and that would be easier if he should lose some of his condescension to her. He had spoken frankly, her sense of fairness acknowledged, though she could wish he had not mentioned the schoolroom and her general ignorance of Society. It would only be sensible to meet him halfway. She faced him, her hands behind her back. "Some of what you say is true," she began slowly, "and what is not I will ignore. At times you have behaved without thought and with abominably bad manners, and while certain considerations might have induced that behavior, you should have had enough force of character to hold to the proper line of conduct."

He looked startled, which pleased and encouraged her. "For my part," she went on, "I must likewise admit that at times I also have not been conciliatory. I might, perhaps should, have overlooked what seemed to me to be deliberate provocation. So, in my turn, I offer you my apologies." At that she held out her hand. "Shall we agree we have both been sometimes in the wrong?"

His clasp was strong but brief. "You are indeed behaving like a gentleman, Miss Minturn. So we will encounter each other amiably and, as I predicted, rub along tolerably well when it is necessary."

She nodded. Even in country clothes he looked elegant and of London, and since he was now at ease she could see he had charm. If only he were at ease more often. He seemed to look down on every one around him except Cousin Susan and Mr. Gifford and, of course, the Alburys. But he was in danger of making himself disliked. He would probably pay no heed to her words, but she should say them. "My lord," she began hesitantly, "there is something I feel constrained to point out to you, for your own sake."

He frowned a little. "Constrained? But then it must be

something for my own good and admonitory. Very well, what is it?"

"Perhaps I should not speak thus, but I would be remiss as an amiable acquaintance if I did not. Last evening, I confess, I enjoyed our discussion of the people we saw on the dance floor. But it was obvious to me, not I am sure to all the others, for you schooled your face for the most part, that you looked down on them all and were only amused by them. But may I remind you that it is among these people you will be spending much of your life? When next you meet them, for the sake of future associations that will be inevitable, could you not soften your manner and use a little tolerance? They will be aware you keep a distance, for that you probably cannot hide, but it need not be an icy and superior distance—for your own sake in the years ahead." She continued to look at him bravely, expecting lightning to descend.

Instead he put one hand up and rubbed his chin. "I do not expect to pass much time here, for I will eventually take a house in town. But since I have an estate, and for other reasons, yes, I will probably be here, perforce. I must allow, Miss Minturn, there is something to what you say. Because of the future, as you mention, I will remember and make an endeavor." He gave her a considering look. "Do you go around giving good advice to all?"

"Indeed, no. That would be horrid. But, sometimes, I do when I feel I should." Relieved, she gave him a mischievous glance. "Perhaps it is a remnant of my time as a schoolmistress."

"No. I should judge it is your good sense, on which we will both rely." They turned and started toward the Hall. "You put one thing out of my mind. Gifford instructed me that I should ask you to go riding with us tomorrow morning. He said you have no one to go out with and is convinced you would enjoy riding beyond the bounds of the estate. Would that be convenient?"

"It would, sir. I would enjoy that beyond anything. Please thank Mr. Gifford for his thought."

"I wasn't going to ask you," he confessed, not looking at her, "for I felt it would not be agreeable, but now I see it would be, so we will meet tomorrow at ten at the stables? Good."

On hearing of some of the conversation, Cousin Susan confessed that the declared peace had relieved her of a certain anxiety.

During tea a note was brought from Lady Erica inviting them to tea the following afternoon. "I trust," said Cousin Susan as she wrote her acceptance, "that we will be invited to other houses. It is presumably from the men you meet here that you will find that husband to enable you to comply with his lordship's will, if you so desire."

"Lord Deveron does not have my problem," Thea said a little sadly. "That marriage can be arranged as soon as desired."

"When he is assured of his share of the Hall. But one can never be sure of a marriage until the rings are exchanged."

"I hope something puts a spoke in her wheel." Thea could but regret his choice, no matter what might be his faults.

The drive to High Wyfells took them across the stream, down a valley, through a tiny village almost hidden beneath elms and lindens to open gates whose pillars supported griffons, and a curling drive. The house was brick and timber with a shallow courtyard and wide windows facing south. Lady Erica was receiving in the Silver Saloon, the aged butler informed them as he led them through two rooms to one that could have no other name. The sprays of flowers on the white panels were done in silver as were the swarming plaster cupids on the ceiling, the rug was silvery gray, and the chairs and tables had received a silver wash. Resolutely Thea refrained from showing surprise, but Cousin Susan laughed. "Erica, so kind of you to invite us. But what is this apartment?"

Lady Erica, in a startling red damask, gave a deep chuckle as she waved them to chairs by the tea table. "So happy you found it convenient to join me. Why, this is copied from Knole, you must know. Some idiot ancestor of Bourne's—it is his house—was overcome by what they call the Silver Room there and did his best to imitate it. Fortunately he realized in time he could not sustain the expense of real silver, so this is a paint or a wash, renewed on occasion, but the effect, it is said, made him quite happy. Miss Minturn, I see you are in top bloom after the festivities. You enjoyed it? No, don't answer, for any girl would. And the people? No, don't answer, for how could you say anything of value after one glimpse—and the inanities you would be forced to utter, for it is evident you are a well-mannered girl, would bore me."

"Tut, Aunt Erica," said an easy voice from the doorway. "You should not permit yourself to be bored by a pretty girl."

"Always am," she retorted. "Different with gentlemen I've always known. Come in, Bourne, and greet our guests and have some tea, though how you can after the large luncheon you devoured I can never understand. Susan, do you still take your tea strong enough to float an egg? You two young ones can have one cup and then remove yourselves to the garden so Susan and I can enjoy ourselves."

Thea wished she could have heard their gossip, but Lord Bourne was settling his long legs and gazing at her reproachfully. "You did not come to admire the stream this morning."

"One cannot go to the same spot every morning," she

protested lightly. "Anyway, I was detained for a . . . a discussion."

"Of your problems, I am sure, and I trust it was enlightening." He lifted his eyebrows and the scar on his left cheek deepened, giving him a sardonic look. "The dance was discussed? You will doubtless find admirable qualities in your neighbors, the more you see of them—fortunately for your purposes."

"What purposes?" Thea asked, not conscious of any.

"Don't pretend to be scatterbrained. Put down your cup and I will show you the yew garden, our chief source of pride."

Their departing courtesies were hardly noticed, and a gleam of amusement passed between them. They went out a secondary door and along a brick walk between enclosing cedar hedges toward a thick green wall that, around a corner, showed an archway. Through that lay a lawn, a garden, full of gently moving figures.

Thea gave a cry and clapped her hands to her cheeks. Two ladies in wide skirts were dipping a little welcome while beside each a gentleman's plumed hat fluttered in his hand. Ahead a wide-spread tail of a peacock shifted and bent. Two griffons stood on guard, and two charging horsemen faced each other across a sundial. The air was filled with a faint rustle and from somewhere came the steady click of pruning shears. "Oh, it is beautiful," she cried and stretched out her hands.

"Yes. Quite a sight." Pride was evident in his voice and smile. "It was started at the time of Dutch William, topiary gardens became very popular then, but they fell out of fashion in favor of the French style. My family liked it, and so we've always kept it." He was looking it over with unabashed affection. "Silly to support a whole family for generations to keep it up, I know. But it was my favorite spot when I was young. Only child, you see, and lonely, and these were friends, particularly that little dragon in the far corner. I told him my troubles and always was convinced he'd rush out and rout my enemies in time of need. Also convinced they moved at night and used to creep out to watch them. They do, too, you know, in a good wind. Quite a sight."

"Why," Thea cried as at a revelation, "you're a romantic."

"Romantic?" A faint red colored his cheeks. "That's by way of being an insult these days. I'll have you know I was an excellent officer and a successful businessman. Nothing romantic about me." He took her arm and drew her to a bench by the sundial. "What do you intend to do now and in the future?" he asked curtly.

"Why, nothing," she faltered, and was pleased with herself for not having said it was none of his business, her first thought.

He snorted and the gray eyes narrowed. "Aunt Erica extracted your story from your cousin. You apparently have some spirit and intelligence, so don't tell me you haven't thought beyond dinner tonight. Here you are under this ridiculous will. By now you must realize Ardsley is worth considerable effort. To keep your share you must marry quickly, and you have spent time in London so now you are of the first stare. Deveron is evidently bespoken. Gifford is paying you some attention. Will you take him and spend your life sharing all you have with the Albury? Did any gallant at that ball catch your fancy?"

Undoubtedly he was trying to disconcert her. An impish thought crept into her mind. She widened her eyes. "Only you, my lord."

She had surprised him. "Gammon!" he exclaimed loudly, but a flush crept up his thin face. "You are trying to embarrass me, and it won't work, my girl."

A gurgle of laughter escaped her. "But I put you to the blush, sir, and for the second time."

"Such impropriety would any one. You are a forward minx. You better be looking over the eligible gentlemen around here. Come. We are being summoned." He rose and put out a hand to assist her. "In case you might feel tempted to try to start a flirtation with me, I should tell you I am not in the petticoat line."

"You have made that very evident, my lord," and she gave him a twinkling glance over her shoulder. They passed between the green ladies and if Thea had been alone she would have curtseyed in response. At the archway she looked back. The low sun was settling shadows around the shifting figures. "It is so lovely," she cried.

He looked down at her curiously. "You really feel that. . . . But I warn you such excessive sensibility is an unfortunate trait in this world, and you must learn to conceal it." She could not think of an adequate set-down so they went to the house in silence.

Lady Erica, Cousin Susan reported, had devoted most of the time to rapid, frank, and often scandalous descriptions of the families with any pretensions and any eligible gentlemen in the marrying way. Thea cringed as she realized her circumstances were so well known and widely discussed, but Lord Stanford had made that inevitable. Obviously she must see and be seen, for a little while, anyway.

So, for a week, she and her cousin dispensed tea to callers and attended pleasantly innocuous dinners, and Thea was agreeable to all and encouraging to none. What she most enjoyed were the morning rides with Deveron and Mr. Gifford. Once they encountered Bourne hacking down a lane and exchanged greetings. Exploring the countryside and villages unexpectedly put them at ease. On the eighth morning, however, Deveron told her, with a regret she believed in part genuine, that the Alburys had removed to London and that he and Gifford were following the next day. She assured him she understood perfectly and gave him a kind smile, adding she also would miss the rides, but he would find much in London to entertain him. Cousin Susan's pointing out that it was inevitable was little solace.

Although the following morning was overcast, and Thea hoped it would pour torrents later, she decided on a walk. The shadows of the great trees suited the gloomy picture she was reluctantly drawing of her future. She dawdled down the ride and was not surprised to find herself at a certain spot beside the stream.

"Stop," said a low voice. "Don't move."

She halted. Nothing happened. Then a line flicked at an angle across the gap that revealed the stream. She craned her neck to see and brushed a bordering bush.

"That's done it. Why couldn't you stay quiet a few minutes? He came twice to my fly and I'd have had him on the third cast and some lively sport." Bourne came around the bushes, set a rod against a tree, and gave her a look that combined irritation and resignation.

"You'd have preferred the company of a trout to a lady?"

"Of course. To any lady. Nothing so enjoyable as a good fighting fish. So, with Deveron gone you decided to look to your other neighbor? It won't get you far."

"I'm not trying to get anywhere," Thea protested more weakly than she intended and sat down on the bench.

"You better begin. Did you find your future this past week?"

"You know I did not. And I don't want to marry any one. But it would be monstrously selfish of me not to marry and so deprive Deveron of his share."

"Talked it over, have you? Or did someone else put that maggot in your head? You've no obligation to get him what he wants." He sat down on the far end of the bench and looked at her contemplatively. His cheeks were no longer gaunt, but the lines and bones of his face made him look a little formidable. "Aunt Erica summoned Tillingbourne but got nothing new out of him. Don't raise your hackles, he didn't reveal your competence. But he is on the trail of the next heirs and is convinced he will find them shortly, in case of need."

"That is when I will go and live very happily with Cousin Susan in Dorset."

"No need to give up yet—many others to look over. So, when Deveron steps off to St. George's, Hanover Square, with the beauty, you'll find a simple country church and a local squire's son and hope you'll be able to keep him from bringing the stable into the saloons and going to sleep over his port, and settle down to spend the rest of your life envying Lady Deveron and quarreling over the rights and privileges of Ardsley Hall."

"You are infamous," she flashed at him, "and trying to depress me into the glooms. My family is excellent and my person is not all that displeasing. I'll not settle for a clodhopper."

"Didn't mean to imply you're displeasing," he protested. "Far from it. But you better find those emeralds; you have no other choice."

"I *will* have. I'll *make*—oh, several for me." The smile lurking in his eyes was aggravating.

"Look around some more, then. It'll be easier for you to snare a husband you can manage down here than in London. That new London gloss you've acquired, manner, clothes, makes a greater impression in the country than in the city. You should be grateful to me for my instructions."

"Oh, I am, my lord," she said sweetly. "Do you always counsel people so for their own good?"

"Not often. But I have an unfortunate sympathy, on occasion for the underdog, and if one can give advice and remain detached, why that is gratifying—if the advice is followed satisfactorily. The thing is not to get involved in any way."

"So you manage people as you wish?" That was an appalling thought.

"Not at all. I merely point out the wisest course to pursue and stand aside. Yes," he drawled thoughtfully, "you are probably sensible not to attempt the London season. You'd be the goal of every gazetted fortune hunter, and you're too green to tell the bad from the worst. You'd end up in a shocking stew and all your own doing."

Thea jumped up. "And you'd look on and laugh like the abominable man you are," she said furiously.

"Nonsense. I won't take the trouble to watch. But, again, I wish you luck."

She wished she had left first, and as she hurried toward the ride wished she had said several things that now occurred to her. But he had made her choices very clear and also clear that he believed she would end by settling for a local husband and a life of frustration. At that thought she began to hurry.

Cousin Susan was in the library when Thea burst in. "Dear ma'am, I hope you do not object. I have told Brewton to have our boxes brought down and sent a note to Mr. Tillingbourne to inform him we are leaving for London."

"Of course, love." Mrs. Farraby chuckled and gave her an approving glance. "I have been wondering how long you would take to make up your mind. What do you intend to do there?"

"You and I are going to enjoy the gaieties of the Season, and I am going to find a husband."

Six

ONLY WHEN they were taking their coffee in the the smaller of the two saloons of the townhouse on their first evening, did Thea remember the one great hurdle of any girl hoping to join Society on her first Season. "Oh, dear ma'am." She put down her cup. "I fear I have done you a disservice. I had quite forgot about Almack's, and the need for sponsors and vouchers there, and the doors it opens. We will get on, I trust, on our own, but will it not be dull for you?"

Mrs. Farraby gave her a wide, reassuring smile. "Do not fear, my love. I was well acquainted with those who are now patronesses—except for the Princess Lieven—when we were all younger. I promise there will be no difficulties."

Nor were there. Notes were exchanged with Lady Jersey and Lady Sefton, delightful calls made, the vouchers arrived, and also the wardrobes designed for town. Thea was assurred a discreet line of mother-of-pearl sequins at the neck ruffle and on the gauze overskirt of the white gown she must wear would not be considered excessive.

"Though the color of your hair is not favored at the

moment," Lucille observed, "it has a sufficiency of gold in the brown to keep it from being insipid, and your eyes are an unusual hazel that will attract approval. The white becomes you, though I understand your distaste for it, and the pastels we have chosen for your future gowns will do even more for you."

Thea comforted herself with the memory of those words as she accompanied her cousin into the large plain rooms of the Almack's Assemblies and moved to the line of patronesses. She felt her color heighten under the open scrutiny of all as she made her curtseys, but maintained her countenance through the ordeal. She was sure no one that evening was welcomed with more cordial affection than her cousin.

Lord Ledgefield was waiting for them and with him a straight-backed, sandy-haired man who was obviously of the military. "Susan, Miss Minturn, how delighted I am to see you and in such countenance. May I present my nephew, Captain Rushdon, on leave from the Seventh?" Whereupon the captain bowed and begged the privilege of the next dance. Thea gave a sigh of relief, at least she had a partner for one dance. And then for the second, a plumed dowager who had quickly joined them, claiming an old friendship with Mrs. Farraby, introduced her son recently come up to town.

Captain Rushdon proved to be unobtrusively expert at the country dance and at ease in light conversation when the figures permitted an exchange. "Greatest luck for my uncle to find Mrs. Farraby," he said once. "He was falling into a lethargy these past months. Nothing was right in the world. Perked up amazingly after he found her and been waiting for her to come back. Says she used to be as good a trooper as any soldier."

"I'm sure she was," Thea nodded and almost missed a step.

Lady Albury, her daughter, Lord Deveron and Mr.

Gifford were leaving the receiving line and turning to look over the dancing. They could not miss seeing her for she was in a front set. Lord Deveron looked surprised, Cordelia's eyebrows went up, and then they were strolling away, as though they had noticed nothing unexpected. It was after the third dance that Deveron came and sought the privilege of her hand and, finding it a waltz, obtained permission for her from Lady Cowper. He performed admirably and assured her she would enjoy all the gaieties, and he would look forward to encountering her; but there was constraint in his manner, and Thea wondered if it was due to the presence of Cordelia or if he had put aside their recent easy friendship. Either thought was slightly depressing.

It was quarter of eleven, and but little time was left for a grand entrance when one was made. First came Lady Erica Hadham in crimson taffeta and four crimson plumes; then a tall and elegant young woman with black hair and large eyes in a pale green silk embroidered in gold; then a handsome young man, obviously her brother; and lastly Lord Bourne, quietly distinguished in the proper evening elegance. Halted by the introductions, he surveyed the room swiftly, then was bowing over the hand of Princess Lieven. He and his aunt were obviously known to the ladies. It was as if a little breeze ran around the walls of the hall as fans were raised, heads bent, and dowagers and mothers asked the same question as Captain Rushdon, now beside Thea to take her to supper, "Who is that gorgeous creature?"

Before Thea could answer, Lord Bourne was steering his two companions straight toward them. "Miss Minturn, delighted to see you. Condesa may I present my neighbor, Miss Minturn, and Captain Rushdon? Miss Minturn, Rushdon, Costanza Condesa de Villamayo and her brother Fernando Conde de Villamayo." It was all very imposing, Thea thought with some amusement and did not look at

Bourne who was asking Rushdon with the ease of an old acquaintance if they could not join for supper, with the addition of Lord Deveron, Miss Albury and Mr. Gifford who were passing nearby.

As soon as they were placed and the men were off for plates the Condesa smiled engagingly at Thea. "It is so kind of Lady Erica to arrange this for us and so soon after our arrival. For so long I have heard of Almack's . . . but it is even more delightful to find a friend so quickly, for I am without doubt you and I will be friends." Her English had only the slightest accent, and her attitude was so warm Thea was almost ready to become friends immediately. "We are on a visit to the Duque de Alcantarina, a cousin. Of course you are wondering how we know Bourne. He will tell us."

When the men returned with plates filled with the usual plain food, Bourne let it be known he and Rushdon had recognized each other from an encounter at some unspecified time and place, to which Rushdon agreed with a grin. Before anyone else could speak the Condesa flashed a smile around the table. "There are two topics of which we must dispose at this, the beginning of our friendships. You are all amazed that the sister of a Conde should have the title Condesa."

No amazement was evident on the circle of politely interested faces. "You conceal it well," she nodded. "Such courtesy I would expect. But I must explain for it is most unusual, an exception, you understand, to the usual custom. Ignorant persons may ask questions of you. It is because our ancestor so distinguished himself by his great bravery in leading the right wing at our glorious victory at Gravelines in 1558. When he returned to Spain our King Philip the Second, who, of course, knew of his deeds, asked him what reward he might desire. Our ancestor, a Conde, of course, replied that his wounds and the honor of serving his King were reward enough.

Philip was not one to laugh, but it was said he smiled
and declared some token of esteem should come to the
family. Henceforth, that all might know of the honor in
which he held it, all the sons and also all the daughters
of the Conde's oldest sons should bear his title down
through all generations. And so we have." There was no
complacency or pride in her explanation, just a simple
statement of fact made for their convenience.

"Oh, I say, how splendid," said Mr. Gifford enthusiastically.

The Condesa smiled in acknowledgment, bent her head
a trifle, then went on. "The other matter that should be
made clear is how we came to be such good friends of
my Lord Bourne. Bourne, tell them of our first encounter."

"To my great good fortune, the Condesa rescued me,"
he obliged, with a little bow to her. "I was out with
General Whitelock, you see, on that unfortunate expedition
to try to get back Buenos Aires. But, unknown to us, a
Frenchman had made the army—and the people—ready
against our return. I took some men ashore to recon-
noiter, there was street fighting, which can be demned
awkward as Rushdon knows."

"He will not tell it properly," the Condesa interrupted,
tapping his arm with her fan. "Be quiet. It is I who will
tell. It was at night. His army, our army, our very shopkeepers and servants were fighting, and we had many
more men, of course. My maid had foolishly run to her
mother's house three streets away to bring her to ours,
which was large and strong. I spied them coming and went
to open a little door. At the instant the street was filled
with soldiers—all kinds. Ours spied Maria, her mother,
me, the open door. Some ran toward us, crying they
would take over the house as a fortress. Maria began to
scream. Lord Bourne saw the trouble and came, so fast,
with some of his men to protect us. There was shooting
around the small street and shouts, and men ran in

opposite directions. One of ours turned and fired, and Bourne was down. His men tried to pick him up, but Bourne told them to make for the boats. Maria and I dragged him in the house and made the door very fast, and we were not disturbed again."

Bourne made a motion with his hand. "I was well out of it. They took the best of care of me, but I was not up and about until after the capitulation and the ships were gone. And no one knew where I was and that is why I was reported dead—an exaggeration, you observe."

"But we had no feelings against the English. We were too proud of ourselves for having defeated them. When he was well, Bourne went into business, since he had some very good ideas, and was so successful we hoped he would stay forever. But he said he had to come home."

"And a devil of a time I had getting here and squaring myself with the War office," he added lightly. "Condesa, would you do the captain the honor of giving him this waltz since Lady Jersey had assured me the regulations do not apply to visiting ladies such as yourself. Then I will find some gentlemen who would be happy to meet you, and ladies for Fernando. Miss Minturn, may I have this?"

Since both the Condesa and the captain looked pleased at the arrangement, Thea rose with them and allowed Bourne to lead her to the floor. "Good of Deveron to set it up so you could waltz," he began as his arm went around her. "Knew you'd be light on your feet. So you changed your mind and came to town. Didn't mean to come myself, as I said, but Aunt Erica got the notion of opening her townhouse and the note from Costanza settled it." They swung around smoothly, and Thea decided he was a better dancer than Deveron.

"After your strictures to me, my lord, it seemed the only thing for me to do, to come to town," she said carefully. "You quite opened my eyes."

"Meant to," he said cheerfully. "No one else would. You must find out where you stand. Rushdon's a good chap, but there'll be fortune hunters, though some may be at a standstill because of the conditions. Most prefer an assured fortune. Remember you two will be the most titillating subjects of on dits for at least two weeks, so exercise great care in your conduct, but enjoy yourself."

Before she could answer, the waltz was over, and he was depositing her with her cousin and off to encounter the Condesa. The captain was smiling widely as he came to Thea. "My gratitude, Miss Minturn, for a most entertaining supper. The Condesa waltzes well and created quite a stir and undoubtedly added to my consequence." He laughed as his uncle clapped him on the back and demanded to know who was the beauty, while over his shoulder she saw Bourne and the Condesa strolling in the direction of Cordelia and Deveron.

Thea was gratified to be told by her cousin on the way home that she had behaved so prettily with the older people that she had won general approval, but was not pleased to learn that Lord Stanford's will had been the chief topic of the evening.

It was also gratifying to receive the next morning a red and white nosegay from Captain Nevil Rushdon and two others, both pink, from gentlemen whose faces she could not recall, as well as a stream of notes and invitations. She and her cousin looked at each other with dismay over the pile.

"We need to consult with someone who is well acquainted—and *not* dear Erica," Mrs. Farraby declared. "We must be certain of the respectability of the invitations we accept. I am sending to Lord Ledgefield and begging him to join us well before tea. He is a friend of the great Whigs, though he does not bestir himself with politics except behind the scenes, and knows everyone."

Lord Ledgefield brought his nephew to pay his respects. There was a pleased gleam in his lordship's eyes as Mrs. Farraby outlined the problem, and he moved them briskly into the library. "I'll go over the notes and I'll give you a list for the future, bound to be more. Can't be too careful." They spent a lively hour with Thea and the Captain, taking down the succinct comments about the writers. Thea thanked the captain for his bouquet, and then was sent into a fit of laughter on learning that one of the others had come from a hedgerow fellow who had been after an heiress for four years, and the other from a young baronet of sound lineage and not a feather to fly with. Tea over, Lord Ledgefield suggested a drive in the Ardsley barouche, and the number of encounters with acquaintances and Ledgefield's comments made the time particularly entertaining.

That very evening a note was delivered begging Miss Minturn to do the Condesa de Villamayo the honor of taking tea with her at 9 Berkeley Square the following afternoon. Thea put it down to the desire to be friends, but as she went up the steps of a handsome older mansion and found Lord Deveron just being admitted, they both evinced surprise. There was no chance to do more than look at each other inquiringly as they were led up a broad flight of stairs to the first floor.

In a red and gold saloon hung with tapestries and crowded with heavy armchairs and tables, the Condesa was waiting with her brother. She was wearing a simple yellow muslin of a shade slightly darker than Thea's and they looked at each other and laughed and any ice between them was broken. The gentlemen bowed properly and were murmuring the right words when a large silver tray and tea service appeared.

The first cup was finished when the Condesa's airy comments on London ceased and her voice became serious. "You are wondering why we have asked you together. Fernando and I have discussed when we should reveal our mission to you and decided it should be done immediately. We have come for the Zamora emeralds."

"Indeed, ma'am?" Deveron put down his cup and crossed one knee, his expression one of courteous interest. "Pray tell us more."

"Of course." The dark curls nodded. "To begin with, there has been a legend in our family—for our mother was a Zamora—of the emeralds. We knew our ancestress had been captured on the high seas by a dastardly Englishman who demanded, and received, a huge ransom and, when she was rescued most daringly, kept her jewels, which was not right. The first evening Lord Bourne dined with us, after recovering from his wounds, he admired the portrait of our mother, and her name was mentioned, and Fernando told the story as we knew it.

"Lord Bourne was overcome with laughter and exclaimed at the vagaries of fortune that brought him to our home. He told us the story as he had heard it. As far as he then knew, the descendant of the pirate, Lord Stanford, was alive, childless, and the emeralds still unfound. After that, we talked of it several times, with Bourne always laughing at the notion they could be discovered. Fernando and I are the last of the branch of our family that came from New Granada to Buenos Aires. We have cousins, it is true, in Spain, in Peru, but we feel that if the emeralds are to return to the family, it must be to us. When we were here as children—when a cousin was Ambassador—we scarcely knew of the jewels and were too young to be interested."

"So that is why your English is so perfect," exclaimed Thea.

"But yes. Two years we spent here, for family reasons and so we might learn your language properly. Our father admires greatly your country and your poets and wished us to know them well. Fernando is destined for the diplomatic service, and I intend to accompany him whenever that is again possible."

Lord Deveron held out his cup for more tea. "You speak our tongue, Condesa, with a music we cannot achieve," he said politely. "May I inquire how you mean to find the emeralds?"

She smiled enchantingly. "I will know where they are. I am a direct descendant of that Condesa."

"But," put in Thea, "they were not hidden until after she had been rescued."

"That is true. But my great-grandmother came from Andalusia—a great lady, but there was always a rumor that she might have gypsy blood behind her somewhere. Gypsies, as you know, often have second sight. That I cannot claim, but on occasion I have known when things would or would not happen. I will feel an emotion when I am at the place where Isabella Maria was imprisoned. With her help I will know the man responsible. As I stand in his home, with her aid, I will peer into his mind and learn where he placed her emeralds."

"Fascinating," was all Thea found to say.

"Fernando and I have no doubts." Her face was animated. "When we arrived here we made discreet inquiries about Lord Stanford, for it had been our intention to write and ask if we could visit his Hall. From our man of affairs we learned of his death and the provisions of his will. Since Lord Bourne was our friend and your neighbor, we addressed a note to him in the hope we might meet you both and, *voilà*, we have, and most sympathetic we have found you." She gave each a dazzling smile.

"But," began Thea, "that would mean your coming to the Hall."

"Of course. We are convinced you and Lord Deveron will wish to assist us in restoring the emeralds to their rightful owners."

"But," Thea began again and more firmly. "Lord

Deveron and I have come to London for the Season."

"That is understood. And we will be enjoying it mightily ourselves. People are so welcoming. But surely you will return to your place at some time for a visit. It is our hope you will be kind enough to include us when you do." She flashed a mischievous smile that said quite plainly, "I know I have you and there's nothing you can do."

"Of course," Thea said immediately. She wasn't going to be put out of countenance by any one. "Your company will give us the greatest pleasure, and it is my home where you must stop since it is where your Isabella was lodged during her unhappy imprisonment."

"That will be most appealing." The Conde spoke for the first time. "We have told no one, you understand, of our purpose in coming. If we fail, no one will be able to laugh. If we succeed, no one will need to know."

"We'll not fail," and Thea thought she heard an echo of some one—was it Lady Macbeth?—and was quite prepard to believe the ringing assertion. But instantly the girl was laughing again, and Lord Deveron was bringing himself up to the finish line by seconding Thea's invitation. After that, all agreed they were looking forward to meeting at Lady Sefton's ball, and Thea and Deveron departed for their carriages.

"We must not be seen conversing here," Thea remonstrated as he paused on the sidewalk. "If you would come to the house in a few minutes we can talk there." As she went to her barouche, she saw with satisfaction his curricle turning in the opposite direction.

Within ten minutes, which gave her time to tell her cousin of the Villamayo quest and go to the small saloon, he was with her. "This is a devil of a coil, Miss Minturn," he burst out as he settled on the sofa and brushed at his hair distractedly. "Of course we could not refuse their visit. Mighty highhanded, I thought it. It will look

devilish queer if we return to Ardsley with these for-
eigners."

"Then we will invite one or two others, as if it were a
house party as well as a repairing lease. And if we are
seen with the de Villamayos here in town, we will be
thought most agreeable to be entertaining them to such
an amiable degree."

"That's all very well to say." His eyebrows were drawn
together, and he was looking annoyed. "You'll be bosom
friends with her, no doubt, and her brother is handsome
enough."

"But not a light conversationalist." Thea tried for a
mild jest, for she had seen behind his irritation to the inevitable irritation of Miss Albury. "I will endeavor to
keep him amused, but you must do your share, for it
would not be at all the thing if only I were involved in
this house party."

He rose and took a turn up and down the room and
returned to the sofa. His expression was still grave but
no longer annoyed. "Miss Minturn, again you are giving
good advice, and I agree with it." He looked at her
seriously. "You are, you know, quite a different girl from
what you originally appeared. That first afternoon I disliked you, as you disliked me." He nodded. "We neither
masked our feelings completely. I was feeling badly used.
I had not anticipated that the coheir would be the school-
girl you looked, and the conditions of the will I found
mortifying. I allowed vexation to overset conduct. Later,
you went out of your way to affront me. We both behaved
badly, as we once agreed, but since then our deportment
has been most proper, and I have found your company
exceedingly pleasant. Also, I believe my fortunes in a
certain direction have improved, so I feel more in charity
with the world. Now we are fellow sufferers in yet another
awkward situation. Your good sense has shown how we
may best deal with it." Suddenly he smiled a little. "We

agreed to deal amiably at a distance. It is my hope we can now be friends and of assistance to each other in this predicament."

"Well spoken, my lord," Thea exclaimed warmly. "I value your frankness. In turn, I agree we must indeed be on an open and friendly relationship."

He rose and bowed. "Pray call on me at any time, Miss Minturn, for we are in this together. We need not rush into it, though."

"They'll not change their minds." Thea's conviction was firm. "We must prepare shortly for the visit." She would need time to see if that problematical husband would come into her life. "We may put the house party out of our minds, but not for long."

Seven

AS SHE contemplated the future house party, Thea glowered at her reflection while Cadwell arranged her hair for a small concert at Lady Mately's. It was Bourne's doing. Not that he had done it on purpose, in all fairness she had to admit that, for he could not have avoided the two Spaniards. Still, somehow, it was his fault, and she wished she could give him a set down.

Since she couldn't, she contented herself with a frosty bow when they passed after the music was at last over, and with flirting with a Sir Hector somebody-or-other who was older and somewhat haggard but making himself particularly agreeable. There was a crush around the dance floor and a voice behind her whispered, "Don't waste time on him, a ramshackle fellow." Then the voice rose. "Miss Minturn, may I present Mr. Salton? He has been pressing me to meet you." Turning as much as the crowded room allowed, she encountered a solemn Bourne and a blond, fresh-faced young man who bowed and eagerly begged the favor of the next dance, to which she graciously agreed. In that dance she encountered Bourne briefly during a slow promenade. "Salton's all right," he informed her. "A sizable competence. You could do worse." He gave her a benign look as they separated. She hoped he would see her the next afternoon, in her new and becoming green habit, riding with Captain Rushdon.

Lady Sefton's ball was of the first elegance, and Thea had to remind herself not to gawk at the glitter of the chandeliers reflected in mirrors, the gold of the window draperies, the vases of flowers, and the gowns of the ladies. She was thankful that she was already acquainted with a sufficient number of gentlemen so she would not be forced to sit out a dance at an affair of such distinction.

Lord Deveron requested the third waltz—the first she saw being bestowed on him by Miss Albury and the second by the Condesa. "Wished to dance with you once," he remarked as they went to the floor. "A pleasure, of course, and we must keep up appearances."

"I am happy you say it is a pleasure, my lord," she rallied him, looking up into the long-lashed blue eyes and chiseled features. "It is indeed obligatory for us to give every appearance that it is. Have you acquainted Miss Albury with the purpose of our Spanish friends?

He bent as if for some confidence. "She said she was amused at the pretensions," he allowed, "but she thought it the outside of enough that they should expect us to bestow those stones, if found, on descendants at such remove. She then waved aside the possibility they would be found. Do you not agree, as I do?"

"Oh, indeed. But it should be a compelling experiment to watch. How particularly handsome both the Spaniards look tonight, they have such an air, and yet are not at all high in the instep," she went on innocently. "It is most agreeable that they show so openly their pleasure when encountering us both."

"And how relieved I am that I have no mansion for entertaining them here in town," he said seriously. "You

are right, however, we must make a show of friendship."
His tone was not happy.

Lord Bourne, claiming her ruthlessly from two peti-
tioners for the last waltz, put it succinctly. "Deveron is
going to find himself in a thicket over the Condesa. Even
one dance displeased the blonde. Tell me what you learned
from Costanza."

"We agreed it should not be spread abroad, my lord,"
Thea said meekly, eyes on the dark blue shoulder before
her.

Somehow he managed to give her a little shake. "Do not
be stupid again. I know their purpose. It is my affair as
well as yours since it is through me they are here. Whatever occurs, you will need my help, you know. We will
revolve in this corner and not come out until I have
heard. Let us both show animated spirits while you tell
me, but do it quickly."

Thea enjoyed the telling for it was agreeable to look up
into the attentive and amused face and quite forget she
had once put the blame for it all on his shoulders. She
was sorry she had to follow his instructions and recount
the ridiculous situation in a few words, but she was aware
the dowagers would not approve of any lingering for
more than a few minutes. She ended with her proposal
she make friends with the two, which he approved, and
brought her back into the crowd.

"How goes your own hunt for that meek husband," he
then asked. "You have numerous requests for dances, and
I am sure bouquets descend daily."

"Why do you say meek?" she asked indignantly.

"Surely he would have to be, for you would not
permit any man to manage your share of the Hall and
would keep as much control of your fortune as Tillingbourne could arrange. Of course, the man will have to
be meek, and it would do well to keep him besotted, too."

"That I could never do." She shook her head. "I

could believe no one who made that claim. But as to managing—that I allow I would try, for it can be most gratifying when successful," and she shot him a mischievous glance. She fell silent and without conscious thought watched Lord Deveron guiding a handsome, middle-aged lady around a not very expert couple, and then around another.

"You are making a plan," Bourne said above her. "You apprehend that when dancing with a gentleman, your thoughts should center on him, but with me that does not matter. Bring back your wandering thoughts and tell me."

"It is solely on your behalf." Again she gave him a sideways glint of laughter, for the two men had given her an idea. "The Condesa desires us to be friends, as do you. So I should find something to entertain her. I doubt if she has ever seen a maze such as the one at Hampton Court, which I have heard praised. Would not a drive there be pleasing and unexceptional?" As she spoke, the possibilities enlarged and she could hardly wait to arrange the expedition. "With a brother and sister there would be no need for a chaperon on an afternoon drive. Lord Deveron could carry Miss Albury in his curricle. Would you favor us by joining us in the barouche?"

"No," he said promptly, "I'll not encourage you in any scheme. Hold on, though. Yes, if I don't come you'll ask Rushdon, so I'd better. Settle the time and I'm with you. Now I must go in search for my own heiress, for I have decided to look over the field."

He smiled blandly at her startled look and planted her beside her cousin and a waiting partner. Thea did not believe his last words, though he was sufficiently wealthy and distinguished to marry wherever his fancy settled, and put them aside.

The afternoon of the expedition to Hampton Court was sunny and not too warm. Lord Deveron, with Miss

Albury looking delicious in pale green, led the way in his curricle. Lord Bourne, in the barouche, seemed pleased that he had an attentive audience of three whom he could instruct on the buildings, the varieties of persons and vehicles encountered, the duels that had taken place on Putney Heath (those two tales had particular success with the de Villamayos), and the beauties of nearby Syon House, for it was all as new to Thea as to her guests. He reminded them that the Court had been begun by Cardinal Wolsey, but his master had so admired it he had given it to King Henry the Eighth before it should be taken from him, and the King had added to it enormously, as had those who followed.

The curricle awaited them by the entrance, with two attendant ostlers. Lord Deveron announced with modest pride that he had sent ahead to bespeak a parlor and a table under an arbor at the adjacent inn so the ladies could refresh themselves now, but tea must wait for their return from the fatigues of the maze.

"Could we not go into the Palace?" asked Thea wistfully while she admired the huge gatehouse across the moat.

"It is quite too large, even the rooms one can visit," Miss Albury said decisively. "It is to be explored only when one is young and the legs never tire. Deveron, do find the maze, for that I have never seen."

"Since it is daytime it would hardly be worth while to go into the Palace, for we would not see any of the ghosts," consoled Bourne.

"Ghosts!" The Condesa gave a little shriek of pleasure. "Those I would dearly like to encounter."

Miss Albury gave her a glance of distaste but before she could speak Bourne put in suavely, "Alas, they—for there are several—appear only in the Haunted Gallery in the night, and visitors, to our regret, are not permitted then, even for the pleasure of seeing two of Henry's Queens."

"But that is stupid," the Condesa said forcefully. "Could not some persuasion be brought? A ghost of a queen would be excessively gratifying."

But Bourne shook his head sadly, and she shrugged and followed Miss Albury while the Conde asked Thea if she believed it all, and she had to allow she did not.

At the opening between the high yew walls Bourne made a wide gesture. "Try your luck, my friends, and see if you can find the center and return. But never fear if you cannot, for I will rescue you." He bowed to the ladies. "Follow your instinct, as will we, and endeavor to meet."

Last of the ladies, Thea turned to the right and turned again, keeping close to the hedge wall which was so thickly grown, expertly trimmed, and high, nothing was visible through or over it, and the paths and corners most confusing. It was quiet and green and peaceful as she walked, and even a little cry of dismay did not disturb her. By still holding to the right she suddenly found herself in a grass-covered circle that held two trees and a bench beneath each, and sat down to wait.

Bourne followed her almost immediately. "Thought I'd find you here, even if you did come by chance and not design." He dropped down beside her. "I'll give them ten more minutes and then get them out, though it's all a hum to say the ladies tire easily."

"How do you come to know the maze so well?" Thea asked, idly watching two sparrows take a dust bath at the base of a yew.

"Had to bring some small cousins here when I was in town after being sent down. Self-protection, purely." His smile was reminiscent. "I do have it written down, the directions, in my pocket if I need it, but I think I'll remember."

Thea turned and examined again the thick dark green hedge behind her. "Since you know the maze," she began casually, "are there not sections that are cut off from all the rest except for the entrance?"

"A cul-de-sac, you mean?" His eyebrows went up. "A few."

A delighted shriek floated from somewhere. "Then," Thea sprang up, eyes sparkling, "find me one. I'll be a noisy ghost. They won't like that by half, but it will give them a delicious fright to talk about. I wish I had chains to rattle," she added regretfully and started toward the opening.

"Come back," he called. "You'll get lost."

"Then I'll turn into a ghost," floated back, and before he could reach the entrance she had disappeared. Laughing in spite of himself he waited and was rewarded by a long rising wail. The merry laughter floating from somewhere stopped abruptly. He started forward just as a series of gulping sobs broke out and were cut off. Quite a different scream rose from another section and a shout. The long sobbing wail mounted to new heights and wavered down.

In only a few minutes Thea ran through the entrance, her face alight. "How did it sound?" she asked eagerly. "I thought it famous myself. Someone screamed, so I must have been good."

"You're an abominable girl and a menace," he said severely but smiled in his relief. "How . . . ?"

"Oh, nanny used to tell me ghost stories, though not about queens. And your map helped," she told him airily and held out the paper. "With a little more time I think I could have found my way."

"You took this from my pocket?"

"Of course—when you were being so self-righteous. But we better find the others for I can hear some very ladylike exhortations to get her out instantly." She turned to leave and began to laugh so hard she leaned against the yews, jumped when they prickled, and laughed again. "Dear Bourne," she gasped, "it is such a long time since I have so enjoyed myself. Lead the way and I will follow."

They came on Cordelia, tottering slowly and leaning on the Conde's arm and, around two more corners, on the Condessa, playing her own version of hide-and-seek with Deveron and proclaiming she must find the ghost. Bourne assured her that one never saw a ghost in the daylight and they must follow him, though it meant going all the way around, of course, if they wished tea. Cordelia ceased to totter but possessed herself of Deveron's arm. Meekly Thea brought up the rear, agreeing with the Conde that the strange sounds must have been an echo from somewhere outside.

During the tea under the arbor the marvel of the maze, Bourne's mastery of it, and the thrill of hearing what had undoubtedly been a ghost, even if it was in daylight, were the chief subjects of a happily prattling Condesa until Cordelia shuddered and begged her to desist, for her nerves were still unsettled. The Condesa, with a wide look of surprise, obligingly changed the subject to inquire how Miss Albury and Lord Deveron contrived to arrive so well in advance and demanded to know how a curricle could move more quickly than a barouche. Without a glance at Miss Albury, Lord Deveron begged her to return with him, reminding Cordelia, stony-faced, that she had complained of the dust his prime pair kicked up when they moved at more than a trot. On the way home the Conde was so attentive to Cordelia, with Bourne interjecting some flattering remarks on occasion, that she unbent before the drive was half over and rallied them with delight. Thea listened and watched and thought of the two in the curricle and laughed whenever there was occasion.

"You did that on purpose," Bourne accused as he escorted her to her door from the barouche. Thea just gave him a look of wide-eyed innocence. "I am wondering what will be the consequences," he added as he left her, after she had thanked him warmly for all he had done to make the afternoon such a success.

Within four days it was evident that Lord Deveron was spending nearly as much time with the Condesa de Villlamayo as with Miss Albury, that the number of admirers around that lady had cautiously increased, and that the number of gentlemen begging for introductions or for dances from Miss Minturn was on the decrease.

"Hoist with your own petard, my girl," Lord Bourne pointed out as he encountered her on Bond Street and turned to walk with her. "The dark beauty is fascinating Deveron. Miss Albury does not care for his defection and is encouraging other admirers, though I doubt if he notices. But the betting is altering at White's, I'll have you know. It's ten to one now he'll make an offer, five to one they'll marry before the time is out, odds were shorter a week ago."

"Are men really betting so—so horridly?" asked Thea, shocked at the thought of the discussions that must precede the wagers.

"Common," Bourne assured her cheerfully. "Some'll bet on anything, two drops of rain going down a window pane, if the next girl to pass the window will be fair or dark. Don't hold with it myself, too chancy."

"Since it is not so certain about Deveron and Miss Albury," Thea said slowly, "that is why I am not so sought after at the moment."

"Of course. Why I said you've hoist yourself. Deveron seems to be hedging off, and what you both get hangs on each other. But you'll find someone. Salton is vastly taken. Rushdon's the best, but he's a wary bird. You become more attractive every week, but be careful what games you play." He bowed before she could answer.

The next evening Mr. Salton confirmed that there was a falling off in the number of her admirers. They were sitting out a quadrille on a sofa in a small alcove and drinking orangeat, which Thea detested, when he removed the empty cups and faced her with obvious determination. His face was white, but his eyes were steady and his bearing dignified. "Miss Minturn, I must speak to you."

"Oh, pray, no, Mr. Salton," she begged. He was a particularly agreeable young man and she was loath to hurt his feelings.

"I must. I have found you the most entrancing lady of my acquaintance, and I am convinced we could be happy. It matters not to me whether or not you inherit that Ardsley. I can support you in good style and that would give me great pleasure." He took a long breath. "I love you, Miss Minturn. Would you do me the honor of marrying me?"

He was so appealing and so serious that Thea wished she had a tendre for him, but she could only shake her head gently. "I am most sensible of the honor you do me, sir, but I truly cannot."

"You must marry someone, they are saying, if Deveron does. You have not shown favor to anyone. May I at least hope?"

"I am not convinced I will marry," Thea found herself saying, "no matter what the consequences."

"But if you find yourself at point non plus and discover you must," he said composedly, "I assure you I will be waiting."

"You are very kind," she told him gently and put out her hand and rose. He bent over it solemnly and walked with her to the promenade.

Cousin Susan was gratified that Thea had received such an advantageous offer, but agreed there was no need to marry anyone unless she so desired and that her income would support her in later years. That thought Thea put from her mind and spent considerable time displaying the sights of London to a Condesa who was so enthusiastic that the expeditions became enjoyable. The Conde escorted them wherever they wished to go, even shopping, and if one of his sister's admirers joined them, he seemed very content to walk with Thea and confide in her how much he missed his own *estrancia*, which he tried to remember to call the family estates, and which apparently encompassed a vast number of square miles. But at times the mortifying thought came to her that her acquaintances—she felt few were friends—were watching and speculating on her fortunes, particularly when she realized that she would surely end up with no fortune, no husband, and no home.

Eight

SINCE THE evening was unduly warm, the long windows of Lady Cranforth's ballroom were open to the terrace from which steps led to an extensive garden below. There the darkness was relieved by torches on pedestals but not so closely placed that there were not spaces where one could linger without being too nearly perceived. Thea had already refused twice to descend to the garden and was prepared to do so again when Sir Hector Neddlesham approached to claim his country dance. He was dressed in a dark brown superfine, with a yellow waistcoat and pale tan breeches; there was gray in his carefully arranged hair above a narrow face and bold brown eyes. She had found she was not attracted to him; but his attentions had been almost assiduous, he was amusing, a good dancer; she could enjoy his company and saw no reason to refuse it in spite of Bourne's words.

The room was crowded and the dance sufficiently energetic to make Thea feel quite warm and bring little beads to Sir Hector's forehead. At the close he led her quickly towards the windows. "It is excessive, the heat here," he said softly. "The parterre will be cooler." The thought of a breeze was welcome, but there seemed to be none wandering by the terrace. One brown arm gestured to the garden. "Away from the house it will surely be more refreshing. Would you not care to stroll for a few moments?"

Though she had refused before, the gentle flapping of her handkerchief brought no relief. "It is not quite the thing," she began doubtfully. But when he took her arm, she accompanied him down the steps and found in the dimness a breeze sufficient to be welcome. There were other couples appearing and disappearing down the pink and blue gravel paths. In a circle of grass rose a single spray of a fountain whose drops reached to the brim of its basin. Thea held out her hands gratefully and laughed. "This is more pleasant than the ballroom," she acknowledged, "but the next dance . . ."

"Your partner will not forget it, but you may in the interest of comfort," he assured her. "There is a spot, here to the left, where it is even cooler and a small fountain where you may dip your handkerchief with no one to notice."

The thought of a wet handkerchief on her forehead was appealing and a reward for not using powder as did some ladies. "Lead on to the water, then, sir," she said brightly, "for I would indeed enjoy a few more moments of coolness."

Again he took her arm and guided her down a small path. If the garden had not been surrounded by a wall, and if there had not been other couples appearing and vanishing in the openings of walks and between bushes, Thea would have hesitated, but it seemed that many of the ball had moved out of doors and it could not be far to where he was taking her. It was only around a bend and between two torches to a little cleared space of white gravel where, on a stepped pedestal, a white pillar with a low gurgling spray rose from the center. High bushes screened the place, and a marble bench waited invitingly. The trickle of water did seem to cool the air.

"Oh," Thea paused, "I'll have to climb up." She hurried to the mounted grass mound and the three steps that took her level with the fountain. Leaning forward, she dipped her handkerchief in the water, wished it was a large towel, and applied it to her forehead and cheeks. This is probably not proper, she thought, and did it again. But that would have to be sufficient, she decided, and dabbed at the drops on her face and wrung out her handkerchief and turned.

"That was most refreshing," she declared gratefully, and found Sir Hector waiting on the mound. She started down the steps, holding out a hand to him. On the last she felt a push at her left foot which overbalanced her, her hand was seized, and she was swept into the man's arms.

"Miss Minturn," he began. "I am deeply in love with you. I know you have a tendre for me already. Pray do me the honor to accept my hand in marriage." His head descended as if to kiss her, but she managed to turn away so the kiss landed on her cheek.

She tried to twist from his hold. "Sir Hector, you are quite mistaken." He held her tighter. "I have no tendre for you. I will never marry you."

"You will when I have finished," he said in quite a different voice and jerked her down from the mound to the path. "It is secluded here. When we enter those bushes no one will see us." One hand went to her dress as though to tear it, came away and caught her wrists together, while the other arm went around her, and he began to haul her towards the bushes.

"I will scream," she warned breathlessly, trying to kick at his legs though impeded by her long gown.

"No one would hear, or care if they did," he growled. "Give over now and say you will accept my hand."

"Never," she said loudly. "Stop this, or I will yell."

Though she could twist from side to side she could not loosen his hold. She opened her mouth to scream and he dropped her hands, smacked her face, and seized her hands before she could raise them.

"Bitch. You'll be glad to have me when I'm through." They were nearing the rim of the circle in spite of her struggle. He paused for breath and still holding her bent and kissed her neck and shoulder. Shock stilled her for a moment, but an instant attempt to twist again was futile.

"Let me go," she gasped and raised her voice. "Help," she cried but despairingly knew her voice had not been loud.

He was stooping a little as though to lift her when a hand on his shoulder swung them around. "The lady seems unwilling," said a cool voice. "Ah, yes. It is Neddlesham. I thought so. Release Miss Minturn." The words were carefully enunciated.

Sir Hector moved a little to face the newcomer. "The lady is not only willing but desirous, Bourne. Leave us."

"Oh, Bourne," Thea cried. "Hit him."

"With pleasure, when you are free."

She saw an open hand descend sideways and violently on Needlesham's upper arm. His hand dropped from hers. Before he could free his other arm from around her, she was pulled away. Bourne was facing Sir Hector, half laughing. "Come on," he invited, "your right arm is still functioning." Neddlesham raised it quickly as though to strike. Bourne's fist took him neatly on the chin, and he crumpled to the gravel.

"Oh, hit him again," cried Thea, clutching a near-by branch. "He, he's despicable."

"Can't hit him when he's down," said Bourne reasonably. "Get up, Neddlesham, and get out. Be glad I didn't blacken an eye instead. If you say anything of this, I will —both of them." He stood balancing and watched the man get unsteadily to his feet, brush at his jacket, stare from one to the other, and walk past the fountain to the path. "That is, I hope, a lesson to you, Miss Minturn, not to play any more little games." Bourne did not look at her.

Still clinging to the convenient branch, Thea gasped in anger and outrage. "What do you mean?"

"I saw you go with him and down the steps, arm in arm, gay as you please. But that's not done. I told you you were too green. Though you've picked up more polish these past weeks you've not got proper conduct in your bones. You're too impulsive, too easily gulled. You'll not find another unmarried girl dallying in the garden."

"That room was so hot . . . the garden . . . he said it would be cooler. I didn't realize. . . ." She was furious at herself for that stupid stroll and at Bourne for making her aware she was in the wrong.

"Just what I told you. You don't know enough to manage. Just thought you'd make others jealous, eh?" His words were not quite so clear-cut now.

"You are outrageous." She straightened, though she still held the branch.

"Not a bit. Saw you in his arms as I came down the path."

"I went up to dip my handkerchief in the fountain," she began furiously, "and when I started to come down the steps he tripped me, caught me."

"And began kissing. Saw that too. That handkerchief tale is too rich and rare. Heading for the bushes, you were."

"Oh. . . ." She let go the branch, took a step to him, and rubbed the wet handkerchief down his cheek. "Now you'll believe me . . . you . . ."

He caught her hand. "Vixen. All right. I believe that evidence. But you'll not deny he was kissing you."

"If you eyes were as sharp as your tongue, Lord

Bourne, you would have seen I was trying to escape his embrace. He never succeeded. I'll have no man kiss me." At the thought her anger rose again. "If I were a man, I'd hit you." She regretted that the torches were not brighter so she could see his face clearly.

"I could see you twisting," he admitted, paused a moment. "So you're still romantic as well as green. You think just because a man wants to kiss you he is enamored of you, cares for you. It doesn't mean that at all. I'll prove that to you right now."

In what seemed like one movement, he pushed her arms down at her sides and caught her to him in such a tight embrace there could be no twisting, and his mouth came down on hers. She tried to move her head, and his hand came up to hold it still. He took his mouth away for a second, and it came down again. Without thought, the first surprise over, she found she was enjoying it and was moving her lips beneath his. There was a long moment and his head jerked up and his hands fell. "Who taught you to kiss?" His demand was harsh and uneven.

"No one. I don't know how . . ." Her hands flew to her face.

"Gammon. Which of the so-called gentlemen have had this pleasure?"

She shook her head, then threw it back. "No man has kissed me before now, I'll have you know." Her own breath was uneven, and the ice she desired would not come in her voice.

"Then you are most delightfully endowed by nature." Though still uneven, his voice had turned mocking. She took a step backward and almost stumbled. "The favorite stumble, eh? But I'll not fall for that." He shook himself to settle his coat and held out his arm. "Come, ma'am. I am returning you to the ballroom." His words were slurring again. As she hesitated he seized her hand and put it on his sleeve, covered it with his other so she

could not jerk it off, and began to walk down the path.
Unless she wished another struggle—and he was undoubtedly stronger than Neddlesham and could stop her
in her tracks—she could do nothing but accompany him.
Very erect, they walked stiffly to the center fountain and
then to the steps.

He—this—was all odious. "I'm not sure I wish to
return," she told him roundly.

"Keep quiet. You can't lose your nerve now. Others
undoubtedly saw you leave the room. You peagoose, you
must return and in good order." He turned and looked her
up and down. "Your hair is in some disorder, but that
could be the breeze. If you'll put that wet handkerchief
in your reticule, you'll show no sign of your . . . encounter. We will enter together and find your partner."

In stately fashion they came through the window.
Never had Thea been so glad to see any one as the
Conde coming to them. "Thank you, my lord, for a refreshing stroll," she said clearly in case any one was
around to hear and inclined her head.

He gave a very small bow. "The pleasure was mine."
He straightened and waited for the Conde.

She danced the remainder of the evening and saw
neither Bourne nor Neddlesham. She wished duels were
not outlawed and Bourne would challenge the man, but
regretfully realized that would not be possible and, in
view of what he had said, he might have no desire to
protect her reputation again.

Inevitably, the scene by the little fountain played itself
over in her mind after she was in bed. Neddlesham she
dismissed with abhorrence; she should have trusted her
first impression, but it was difficult to refuse a man of
good address whom one frequently encountered. But
Bourne . . . his landing that pleasing leveler had been
highly satisfactory, but after that his conduct was in-
explicable, and in the end she concluded he had been

well above himself, which was lowering.

She had no engagements the next afternoon and was looking for something to read when the butler at the doorway coughed and said, "Lord Bourne is calling, ma'am," and stepped aside as Bourne strode in.

His outfit was complete to the height of fashion and his manner assured, though his eyes looked a little heavy. "You are coming to drive in the park with me," he told her briskly. "Go change your gown and be quick about it."

"Why should I, my lord?" she asked with awful formality. "I was not forewarned of the honor."

"Of course you weren't. Don't be hen-witted or take that tone. You are coming with me because I can lend you contenance and forestall any gossip that might start over your being in the garden so long with Neddlesham. Also it is the only place we can talk with a little privacy. Go and be down in ten minutes. I won't have the horses kept standing."

"I'm not one to be ordered," she began, but at the dangerous look he gave her she altered to "so kind" and nearly ran from the room.

Though she kept scolding herself that she should not be so without spirit as to obey the man no matter how threatening his gaze, she rushed into a primrose gown and matching bonnet and, since her blue kid boots would take too long to lace, she went into blue low shoes, snatched up a blue reticule and was downstairs as he was pulling his watch from his waistcoat pocket.

He nodded approvingly. "You can be quick when you wish to be. You look quite the thing. Come along now." But he did not take her arm or offer her his hand until he helped her up to the seat of his curricle.

That he made no attempt to elicit her interest in any topic as they drove to the park annoyed her, and she made no attempt to follow a lady's line of duty and entertain him since she could hardly bring up their last encounter, which occupied her mind. Once in the park, and with no carriages nearby, he began abruptly. "One of the reasons I came for you this afternoon is to apologize for my behavior last evening."

It was, of course, what any gentleman would do. "You were above yourself," she told him, with what disdain she could muster.

"Above myself!" He gave a bark of laughter that startled an elderly lady in a passing landaulet. "I was more than fair and far out. I was bosky. Didn't know what I was doing."

This was not flattering. "Indeed?" she asked icily. "You appeared to know when you knocked down Neddlesham."

"Was almost stone sober then," he said, as if proud of that accomplishment. "Was so shocked by your behavior everything was in order at that moment. I saw I had to help you, after a minute there, then had to get rid of the fellow. You should have known he was a loose fish, not to be trusted," he went on severely. "Told you he was ramshackle. You should never have encouraged him."

"I didn't encourage him." Indignation made her voice rise and he looked at her reprovingly.

"Don't scream like that in the park."

"I'm not screaming. His manners could but be approved. I do not know how to refuse to dance when a man makes a request."

"Your trouble is you're green. I told you how it would be. You don't know your way around. Well, if I see you taking up with any more gazetted fortune hunters, I'll tell him you've lost it all."

Thea thought it safer to ignore that and reverted to something more important. "But if you were sober when you hit that man, how can you say you were foxed?"

"The drink came right back on me. I knew I was over the limit and went out for some air. Forgot fresh air's the worst thing at such a time. But I'd seen you go out, had some thought I should look after you. A man gets these queer notions when he's been dipping rather deep, you know. I saw you go down that side path and decided it a cork-brained thing for you to do and I better pull you out."

"And I'm very obliged to you, my lord." The sincerity in her voice made him look down at her in surprise. "I was at the end of my forces for I could not kick him really well because of my gown. I do not know what he had in mind except that it would have been horrid, so I was very glad to see you. But," she went on carefully, "you were apologizing for being bosky, your word, sir."

"That came next. The pleasure of that facer I landed must have gone to my head and taken the drink with it. I'd never have kissed you if I hadn't been disguised. I'm apologizing for that now."

She froze. "There is no need. You make yourself quite clear that I am repulsive to you except when you are under the influence."

"No, not repulsive at all. Said that once before. In fact, I thought that tawny-colored gown very becoming, with your hair you know, and regretted you did not have aquamarines to wear with it—unusual, but they'd have set you off well."

A memory came to her. She switched around in the seat and looked at him with awful suspicion. "This is another of your play-acting bits, like the night in the Long Gallery. I do not believe you were disguised at all. Which makes your behavior, after you rescued me, all the more odious."

"Again you wrong me. I had certainly drink taken. All the adjectives for that state—so many delicate shades of meaning—never can pick the right one. I undoubtedly was above myself."

"In that state a man cannot be held responsible," she

allowed loftily. "There will be no need to mention it again, or for us to encounter each other except of necessity."

He gave a low hoot of laughter. "There you go," he said triumphantly. "Flying into the tree tops. Knew you would. Another reason I brought you out. You can't afford to stand on points with me, my girl. Nor," he added thoughtfully, "can I with you. We're in too much together, particularly with the de Villamayos. They're my responsibility, but your house is their goal. Costanza's going to look for those confounded emeralds one way or another. It doesn't matter how we feel about each other, we must get along together. You can't cut out them, or me, now. Make talk you can't afford. So we better cry quits and forget what happened."

Thea would have liked to say her nerves were at such a point of agitation she could not contemplate anything he was suggesting but knew he would not believe her as it was not true. For a moment she rebelled at the notion of being so chicken-hearted and obeying him again. But second thought told her he was speaking sense. "I fear you have the right on your side, sir. I shall endeavor to behave with all propriety where you are concerned and forget last evening."

"Don't forget so much you let that hedgerow fellow come hanging around again, though," he added complacently, "I doubt he will. But don't even look as if you remembered that leveler when you see him, or anything else. Bad form. I see it's my duty to warn you of others, though, and to guide your conduct on occasion. And don't say too kind when you don't mean it by half. But come to me if in any trouble." He looked down and held out his hand. "Shake." He commanded imperiously. "Last night is forgotten and never to be mentioned."

It was somehow comforting to feel that warm firm

grasp and to know she could turn to him if there was need. "Now we can discuss the weather and the people," she said brightly.

"Now we'll let out the horses a little and you'll find some better topics than those or I'll set you down." He glanced down again, an odd glint in his eyes. "Knew you'd understand if I explained everything," he said kindly. "You're not always a goosecap. Be prepared to bow to the approaching barouche. I'll help when it comes to my friends. And don't ask me in for tea now for I am engaged."

He was lightly amusing about how dull life could be made for a non-betting man all the way back to the house. Thea was relieved she did not have to entertain him for she felt her wits exhausted. She found she rather regretted again his insistence that he had been so thoroughly foxed when he had kissed her, but she knew men were not responsible at such a time and their actions must be overlooked. Bourne could always get around her, make her change her feelings, her very thoughts, and always with such overwhelming reason. It would be well not to tangle with him in the future, and she must always be grateful to him for his rescue.

The next noon a note came from Lord Deveron asking if he might take her driving and begging her to put off any other engagement. Thea had rather hoped Captain Rushdon would call for he was a most agreeable companion, but she put on a new gown and was waiting when the curricle arrived. Lord Deveron thanked her for granting him her time, handed her up, told the groom he was not needed, and turned his blacks toward the park.

"It's early, I know," he explained, "but, dash it, no chance to talk to you in private." His brows were drawn together, and he looked a little careworn.

Since this was only the second time he had favored her

in this fashion she was elated, and regretted the early hour. That Bourne and Deveron wished to talk to her in private was gratifying no matter what they had to say. She folded her hands over her reticule. "What is it you wish to say, my lord?" she asked quietly.

"Time you called me Myles," he said absently, dropping his hands so the blacks could canter on a deserted stretch. "I think of you as Thea, now. We're not really cousins but near enough for that."

The unaccustomed speed was exhilarating, and Thea waited until the pair were pulled to a trot and gave him a glowing look. "That was splendid," she exclaimed happily.

He gazed at her a moment. "Gifford was right." He sounded surprised. "He said you looked different when you were pleased or on your high horse. I've seen it before, but not so clear as now. Yes. Well. You and I are in a basket." He pulled the pair to a walk and half turned to her. "Know what I mean?"

To have him looking at her so appealingly was as exhilarating as the canter, but she would not help him. She gave him her wide-eyed innocent look she found useful on occcasion. "In what way, my lord?"

"Myles," he said absently. "It's about the demned will and the Hall. Don't mind dividing the place with you, now we're friends, but there's that marrying clause. Must if we're to have the place. Well, wouldn't easiest thing be to marry each other? Nothing said in the will about children being necessary. Each of us could do as we wish, and we'd have the place and then could get divorced whenever we wish. Any number of people get divorced these days."

Thea looked away from the fine blue eyes, now so concerned. This was incredible. But she didn't want it this way. "Forgive me," she began carefully, "but—Miss Albury?"

He gave his shoulders a hunch and looked both hunted and abashed. "Awkward, I admit. Thought I knew what I wanted. So beautiful. I know—I singled her out, paid her particular attentions. But, demmit, I never made an offer. Now not sure I want to, or what I want. Lots of the world left to see," he ended vaguely.

"But will she not be embarrassed before the world?"

"Oh, not that serious. Others always hanging around her, new one just joined them. She'll come about. What do you say?"

What could she say? It was distressing and comical at the same time. There must be a way—she thought fast and found it. She turned her head and smiled. "It is certainly an ingenious notion, my lord. It would overcome all our difficulties. But . . ."

"You've not fixed on anyone have you? Not my concern, of course, but if you have . . ."

"No, of course not." She was thankful her composure was not easily disturbed. "Your suggestion is something to ponder, and we need not settle our course of action now. There is one thing you may have forgotten. We promised the de Villamayos to take them to a house party at Ardsley. Do you not think we should do that before determining any solution to our problems?" She waited tensely.

His face cleared and there was warm approval as he glanced at her. "By Jove, yes. Had forgotten that. You're bright as a button, Thea. We'll do that. Right away."

She felt the tension leave her. "Whom do you wish to invite?"

He flicked the blacks into a trot and bowed to a passing phaeton, for the park was filling. "Those two, of course, and Gifford."

"Would not Miss Albury feel it a slap if she were not included?"

His smile vanished as he nodded. "Undoubtedly, since

she has been concerned for so long. You'll have to get Bourne to go down to his place, they're his friends. You'll want Rushdon, no doubt." He stopped and thought and guided the curricle around a slow-moving landaulet. "Tell you what. I'll keep the men in my part, you keep the ladies. Costanza'll want to be where the emeralds were. That way we're not always in each other's hair. You agree? Splendid. I'll take you back now so you can start writing notes for, let's see, there's the Cooperthwaite ball, every one'll want to go to that, and a drum the next night. Make it a week from today. Give you time to send word to Tillingbourne. I'll fix up the transportation. We'll get this over and done with and then see how we go. And I must say you're a very good sort of girl, Thea."

She found a sharpened quill and a sheet of paper for the note and looked at a French print of a bouquet of flowers hanging on the wall beside the desk. Flowers . . . gardens . . . Ardsley. She sat back. Deveron, so handsome and so engaging when he wished, had suggested they marry as a way out of their difficulties for, practically, business reasons, and without affection, just approval. She had never thought that possible, only that he deserved better than Miss Albury. She *was* better than that statue, she knew. If she were missish she would have been put out of countenance at his frankness in saying it would be only for convenience. Of course he did not love her. She had been dazzled by him from the beginning, in spite of his arrogance, but had come to like him after he came down from his high stirrups. But such an arrangement as he proposed, even if not for long, as he had implied, would be difficult to sustain if she did not love him. Did she? She did not know, was surprised by her doubts and accepted them, so apparently she did not. Had she been truthful in saying she had a tendre for no one? She nodded at the flower print. No one had caught her fancy. She preferred Captain Rushdon as a companion, a most amiable one, and enjoyed his friendship, which was an entirely different matter. There was the enigmatic Lord Bourne whose chief feeling for her seemed to be exasperation which aroused only irritation in her.

But, back to Deveron and Ardsley. Was she sufficiently fond of the place to wish to live there forever, or even for a few years? It was so *large*, though she realized it was small compared to such mansions as Chatsworth or Holkham or Wilton. She shook her head, she did not know. Perhaps the few days—she hoped they would be few—with the guests would show her her true feelings about Ardsley at least. She leaned forward and began, "Dear Mr. Tillingbourne . . ."

Nine

BY USING a variety of vehicles the removal of the house party to Ardsley Hall was accomplished with less than normal difficulty, and changing from one carriage to another after the stops for luncheon and early tea offered a pleasing diversity of travel. Lord Bourne was taking himself off alone to High Wyfells, which Thea had commended. Mrs. Farraby had said, only half laughing, that for her the visit would be too dull to be borne without someone to entertain her, and she believed Lord Ledgefield would be pleased to accompany his nephew, as indeed he was. Since there had been five days' notice Thea had no concern about the state of readiness of the Tudor wing and trusted Mrs. Brewton to oversee the other house as well. On arrival she was informed boxes and servants had arrived and been distributed and dinners would soon be ready at both houses. All agreed it would be desirable to separate now and meet the following morning after a late breakfast.

Both de Villamayos professed admiration for the gatehouse and the ensemble and looked forward to their exploration. On her way to her own room Costanza requested to be shown the room the wicked Sir Richard had used and was satisfied by a glance into Thea's bedroom. The supper in the morning room was unexpectedly pleasant with the conversation kept lively by Costanza's questions about the people met in London and the countryside through which they passed and her evident interest in all she was told. They wondered how the men were faring and whether they had turned to whist for amusement and vowed such effort was beyond their own strengths. When the others had retired, Thea and her cousin agreed that, since there was nothing to conceal, the Spaniards be told they could go anywhere and examine anything as they wished, but Thea was to be consulted if any panels or hearthstone, pictures or chests, were to be moved.

The gentlemen arrived before breakfast was completed and yielded immediately to Thea's urging to have another cup of coffee and then finished all that remained of the muffins, creamed sole, and fried ham. Thea announced the rules under which her house could be explored, which all felt reasonable.

"Jove, yes." Lord Ledgefield leaned back and gazed around the dining saloon. "Couldn't touch that old linenfold without damage. Rooms look remarkably well with it all painted white. Sound notion."

"But anything might be concealed behind panels," objected Costanza.

"Doubtful. But if one's been taken up and put back the marks will show, so look along the edges. Mustn't touch the plaster ornamentation either, those green leaves up the sides of the chimney there, for instance, same sort of thing in other rooms, garlands on the ceiling, nor wall panels, though they're mostly painted. If nothing's marred, nothing's been hidden. Doubt if chimneys have been touched, usually left alone, except for cleaning, even if decorations added. Glad I'm not looking for anything except, Mrs. Farraby, the pleasure of inspecting the gardens in your company." He gave a little bow and a twinkle.

When they had all departed to start the search, Thea went to congratulate the Brewtons on the ease with which the invasion was being handled, to tell the head gardener the cut flowers in the rooms were a credit to him and to Ardsley, and to the stable to inquire if all was well with the horses and sufficient room and help for the additions. On the way back she turned into the rose garden to admire the red and white blooms and approve a new border of lavender around the sundial.

There she straightened quickly as a mocking voice said, "Quite the mistress of the Hall you've been play-acting this morning." Lord Bourne, hatless and in riding clothes, was watching her with the quizzical expression she had seen before and loathed.

"It is no play-acting," she asserted with dignity. "I know from my mother and our home in Devon, small as it was, how a house of any size should be managed and the duties of its mistress."

"Do you now?" There was a flash of surprise. "How unfortunate the time for you to exercise those talents is so short. Well, you had better go to the attic even though that is outside your regular duties for your guests are being vastly more entertained there than by poking into corners which, I gather, are admirably free of dust."

"I'd like to know how you always are aware of what is happening here. How do you keep track of us? It's not your business what we do and I, for one, resent your surveillance."

He threw up a hand as if in horror. "Not surveillance, Miss Minturn. I am shocked beyond measure you should use that word. What a thought for a gently nurtured fe-male, and beyond belief she would accuse a gentleman of such intent. You show, I fear, your lack of understanding of the network of communications among servants achieved by chance encounters in the village, exchanges with shopkeepers and even more frequently over a pint at a pub, and what it is felt they should know tactfully conveyed to the families."

Such activities had never crossed her mind. "How shocking! Is there no privacy?"

"Not from servants in a well-ordered household, so you better remember, for no housekeeping skills can counteract that. Why, I'll wager you don't know one of your upstairs maids is niece to the wife of the owner of the Rose and Crown, the nearest pub, and visits there frequently." He chuckled gleefully. "Come, Miss Minturn, perhaps you couldn't know but you might have suspected. And before you ask me why I am here this morning—I came to join whatever entertainments were taking place. My invitation came from Deveron and was all inclusive. It was Brewton who directed me to the attics and to the gardens. But I won't keep you now. You better go keep an eye on your guests. Don't look at me so crossly. I'm just being useful. It would be becoming, you know, to invite all the gentlemen to dinner tonight."

Thea was shaken by the revelation of what she must expect and ignore, but she could not let that last pass. "You are kind to remind me of my duties," she said coldly. "I had already thought of dinner."

"Don't try to flummox me. You wouldn't have looked so startled if you had. Your friends have enjoyed the morning and found nothing and will want a change for the afternoon . . ." He paused and looked at her seriously, the well-shaped mouth no longer curled. "You and Deveron are friends now, aren't you? He's a good chap, and as intelligent as he is handsome, when he doesn't get himself in a tangle. He may take the easy way out yet, if he's pushed too hard, however; most men would. Count on me for dinner, earlier if needed." He raised his

riding crop in a half-salute and laughed as she walked by
him, head high.

The attics, at the top of the right-angled arm that made
one side of the E that was the Hall, was awash beneath the
beams with silks and velvets and taffetas of red and blue,
white and yellow, purple and brown, all in many shades.
There were gowns with ruffs and paniers, aprons and
trains, while uniforms of red and blue lay on top of silk
breeches, shirts with lace jabots, court costumes of velvet
and damask. Costanza, with a scarlet shawl over her
yellow morning dress, would have charmed the most
aloof gentleman. Even Cordelia was wearing with aplomb
an immense straw hat covered with flowers of every hue.

As Thea appeared Costanza cried, "Dear Miss Minturn,
see what we have found. They are all so lovely we are
quite entranced and have forgotten our search."

"Not quite," objected Fernando, looking up from a
pair of spurred boots he was admiring. "We have gone
over this wing, as we thought it unlikely a hiding place
would be in this secondary area. Next we will concen-
trate on the main house."

"Very sensible," Thea approved. "But I must tell you
that a luncheon is ready at each house. And I hope you
gentlemen will favor us for dinner tonight."

All began to lay aside whatever they had been admiring
amid enthusiastic acceptance from Deveron. "We'll never
get these replaced," Cordelia pointed out with a little
moue.

"By all means leave the things as they are," Thea told
them, and led them down narrow stairs, then wider stairs
and so out on the parterre. Thea started to ask if they
had been to the Long Gallery but refrained, hoping all
had forgotten, as she had.

Costanza, her hands clasped before her, eyes glowing,
exclaimed at the beauty of the trees and hills. "One morning, delightful as it was, in the house is sufficient. Dear

Miss Minturn, would it be possible to ride this afternoon and see a little of this so beautiful land?"

"Just the thing," agreed Captain Rushdon heartily. "Deveron, can you mount us all?"

"Nice idea but pretty tame country," Mr. Gifford said sadly. "Now if we were in Scotland . . ."

Miss Albury, her hair smooth, her dress undisturbed, said gently, "Pleasant as that sounds it is my duty to go and call on my grandmother at Casons. I could not be so near and fail to pay my respects. Deveron, you have been so frequently at our home you will wish to do the same. Shall we use your curricle? At three, then?" She gave him a coolly appproving smile.

Looking a little bewildered for a moment, Deveron nodded. "We can mount you. I'll send word to the stables and Bourne." Slowly he turned to his own wing followed by the other men. Mrs. Farraby and Lord Ledgefield, strolling on to the parterre, declined any part of the exercise.

At the luncheon in the morning room, the Condesa advanced the suggestion that the three young ladies should be on first-name terms. "I know it is not customary to do so on such short acquaintance," she allowed, "and in my country we are more formal than yours. But here one is so at ease, all is so agreeable, one feels all are friends, could we not?"

Miss Albury looked doubtfully at Mrs. Farraby but that lady laughed and nodded. "I see no reason why you should not. It is often done by some of the most starchy ladies. I like it and shall do the same." Costanza clapped her hands with delight.

Lord Bourne rode up to the stables as they were mounting and surveyed them with approval. "All in fine style. Mind you keep me in sight, or you'll be lost in the lanes and miss your dinner, perhaps your bed. Costanza, Fernando, you must ride on the roads, no leaping hedges, fences, ditches, galloping across fields, our farmers don't like it, and you don't know this country." On the way down the drive he reined by Thea. "Are you up to it?" he asked quietly.

"I don't know." She had to be honest. "I've only had those few morning rides with Deveron and Mr. Gifford since the moorland ponies."

"You'll do. Or I'll find you and bring you home in disgrace. Here we go," and he was cantering ahead.

It was the fastest, most exhilarating afternoon of Thea's life. The Spaniards were superb riders and well mounted and went only at a walk when compelled to rest the horses or pass through a village. The rest of the time they cantered or, on a straightaway, pounded into a gallop, pulling off and waving their hats and shouting. Thea found herself shouting too and wished it could go on forever. But Bourne brought them back neatly to a late tea and even complimented Thea, as he passed her, on her seat and spirit.

Thea feared that whatever followed that afternoon would be found dull, but all were in high spirits. The dinner was simple, with only two removes, but with such a constant replenishment of every dish that she realized Mrs. Brewton had long experience with the appetites of gentlemen. Costanza was bubbling, and after dutifully praising the horses and the landscape, and remarking on the oddity of always riding on roads, and telling Deveron he had missed the most enjoyable ride of his life, launched into an account of the family *estancia* and the open miles of land for cattle and the exploits of the gauchos who herded them. Her vivid face and enthusiasm held them all, and Thea was pleased when Deveron rather sharply told Cordelia not to be missish when she exclaimed in horror at the description of a barbecue on the pampas. Abashed, Costanza regretted she had been disturbing and fell silent. Whereupon Fernando launched into tales with spirit and color.

At the close Bourne asked Costanza what she thought of the portrait of her ancestress, and after coffee they moved up to the Long Gallery. In spite of the candelabra Brewton had sent up, the room was dark and shadowed. Costanza gazed at the portrait and shuddered.

"She is beautiful, is she not? Oh, he was wicked. No, I do not wish to see more now. He was clever, also. What of the gold of the ransom, which we do *not* seek?"

"No one knows," Deveron said. "It was said some went for business, some to redecorate the house, new rugs, plasterwork by Italian artists. He enjoyed watching them so much he took to painting, a little. But it was never known how much gold there was or whether it all went."

"Scelerat," said Costanza firmly.

Deveron moved with the candle to the portrait beside the door. "This poor girl was his wife. She looks sadder each time you see her."

Costanza gave one scornful glance. "A poor paltry thing she is, too. Let us go to your spinet. I will sing songs of my country and remove from our spirits the gloom of this room."

She approved of the gold and white saloon and went to the spinet. "I will sing a song of our gauchos. It is perhaps fortunate," she added thoughtfully, "that you do not understand the words." Her contralto was round and warm and fitted what seemed a fiery love song. In the middle Bourne burst into laughter, choked, and subsided under the singer's glare. She sang another—shorter, more lilting. "Though it is to be deplored that I have neither castanets nor heels, I will dance a little for you." She threw back her head, curved her arms upward, gave a stamp though the sound was soft, and twirled, her skirts flying as far out as they could, her arms moving. But almost immediately she stopped. "Bah. It is nothing. I must apologize for wasting your time. You must come to visit us to see it done properly, or go to Spain."

She laughed and tossed her head at their applause and waved a lace handkerchief around her face. Deveron sprang over to open the windows more widely and she strolled to his side, while Cordelia's smile became fixed. Thea moved around with the others and tried to think what would entertain them when Mr. Gifford gave a bang on the piano.

"Miss Albury has consented to sing us some English songs, nothing better." After protesting demurely that they would be very tame in comparison, she allowed herself to be urged to the spinet. As she began to inquire in a light, trained voice who was Silvia, Thea felt her hand seized and she was drawn from her chair at the back to the door by a tiptoeing Costanza.

"They will not notice," she whispered. "It has come to me that I must go for a short while to the room where Isabella Maria was imprisoned. I do not ask her anything now, just tell her I am here, and wait. Perhaps it is too soon. But I must try."

"Of course," Thea sympathized. "I'll show you the way." On the ground floor she lighted one of the candles. The door to the tower stair opened silently. "We are told the lady was kept in the room on the third floor," Thea said matter-of-factly. "It is empty, but there are stone benches beneath the windows. Do you wish a light?"

"You are good and kind." The voice caught. "No light. There will soon be a moon. I must be alone."

"Of course," Thea agreed again, "but I will set this candle on the bottom step to guide you."

There was a murmur and the crimson gown began to move slowly up the twisting, narrow staircase. Thoughtfully, Thea returned to the saloon—fortunately just as Cordelia was saying she could sing no more—and rang for the tea table.

To her surprise it was Deveron who took the chair beside her, sipped and put the cup down and looked at her. "You're a deuced comfortable girl, Thea. You don't fuss. A man feels easy with you." He ate two cakes gloomily, looking out the window. "Why aren't all girls like that?"

She could not repress a gurgle of laughter and saw Bourne, just beyond Deveron, raise his head quickly and look at her. "Because we are all different as you well know ... Myles."

"Dear Miss Minturn—Thea, that is," Cordelia raised her voice a trifle. "We are talking of tomorrow. We may indeed devote the day to the search?"

"As all of you wish," Thea said swiftly. "I will instruct Brewton he is to be at your disposal." A portrait of a shrewd and commanding Lord Stanford in his scarlet uniform hung over the fireplace behind him, the combination brought inspiration. "My Lord," she began formally, "as I collect, we are to have the pleasure of dining with you tomorrow."

"That is the arrangement." His look was wary.

"Food won't be as good as yours, though," Mr. Gifford put in regretfully.

She moved in her chair to face the others. "I am going to suggest that, if it meets with your approval, we all come to dinner tomorrow in costume. There are those gowns and uniforms in the attic . . ."

It was very evident each one instantly saw the many advantages of costumes, and all began to speak at once of what had been found. It was a brilliant notion but, it was agreed, they must choose together so no one would have an advantage.

"Charades and guessing games are quite the thing, you know." Cordelia's voice could carry well when she wished. "At large houses, Chatsworth, Woburn, Longleat, the guests sometimes write their own plays and perform them. But," the smile was kind and a little pitying, "we are so few and our time is so short . . ."

She had reduced Ardsley and the party practically to an afternoon affair for children. Annoyed, Thea was searching for an answer when Lord Ledgefield said roundly. "Better this way. Fatiguing to try to guess what you don't want to know anyway, and worse being polite when your friends and enemies make fools of themselves."

"You are being unkind, Ralph," chided Mrs. Farraby, though she made the word sound admiring, and smiled.

"Not at all. True. There're other ways for an evening of fun. Remember once playing follow-my-leader all over Wilton, at night. We had candles, following Bedford on his first visit. Took all evening. He got lost and so did most of us. The dowager didn't approve, said it was too hard on the ladies, going up and down all those stairs. But you didn't see many ladies on the stairs. Splendid evening." He beamed at Mrs. Farraby. "Wish you'd been there, my dear."

"Just as well I wasn't, for I'd have been exhausted by the stairs," she answered a little tartly.

"Nonsense. I've not forgotten the high spirits you had on occasion." His smile widened. "Too bad it can't be done here—but costumes are enough. Nothing to figure out. There was another time . . ."

"Uncle," Captain Rushdon interrupted firmly, "there is no knowing where the next time will lead you and us and before you know it you will be embarrasing the ladies."

"Not a bit of it, my lad. They're tougher than you think, but," he chuckled, "you're right. I'll save it for Susan."

As she was laughing Thea saw Costanza just outside the door and went to her. The great black eyes were tragic. "There was nothing. I had hoped. I waited. No feeling came to me. Now I go to bed." She kissed Thea's cheek lightly and was gone.

As though the impulse had been catching, the party was breaking up when Thea rejoined it, and she felt it was not too soon.

Ten

IT WAS decided at breakfast that it was of prime importance to choose the costumes for the evening so the maids would have time to press and mend. The rest of the day could then be devoted to the search. But nothing could hurry the gentlemen until all the breakfast serving dishes had been emptied.

"Nothing in my attic," Deveron told Thea as they stood by one of the low windows in hers. "I went and looked and there's just boxes of papers and broken furniture. All the family clothes must be here."

Looking over the gay piles, Thea said, "Yes. And how large the family must have been, and how sad it diminished to really nothing. You and I hardly count."

He looked impressed. "Never thought of it like that. True. Must have been in Stanford's mind when he made the will. Hey, Rushdon's going after something I want. Forgive me," and he leaped over a box to seize a plumed hat.

By the time the ladies had tried on and chosen their gowns and the men had borne off their selections, luncheon was ready and the gentlemen had reappeared. They all vowed to tap, lightly, every panel and moulding and floor-board and gently try to turn every carved or plaster fruit and flower on the two floors. Thea left them to it. Even though Ardsley was not hers, this careful search affronted her, and she went for a walk around the lake. Again, she would try to think of her problems. But the soft breeze, the lapping and sparkle of little waves, the varieties of bushes and trees and changing vistas induced her mind to wander over the past as well as the present. Finally, she laughed at herself and abandoned all thoughts of plans except that she would surely enjoy living in Dorset, for obviously her case was quite hopeless. She would return to her role of hostess and gather what enjoyment she could from these last weeks.

A golden light was fringing the line of trees on the up-land to the west as the ladies stepped sedately along the parterre to Deveron's terrace, a light that gave faces and the stuff of the gowns a glow and vividness. The gentle-men were waiting in a cluster that broke and turned, and each group stared at the other with frank admiration.

"Why, you are more beautiful than ever," cried Mr. Gifford, for once saying exactly the right thing. In re-sponse each lady made a deep curtsey and, with some pride, rose from it without too much visible effort as the gentlemen swept the grass with their hats.

What fun, thought Thea, they all do look more hand-some than usual, and so pleased with themselves. Cordelia, in a blue satin with a full skirt and white ruff and a blue cape that fell into a small train had, thanks to the sunset, more color than usual in her cheeks. Costanza wore figured ruby red taffeta with small hoops and a gold stomacher laced in front that made her waist look very small indeed. Thea, knowing she couldn't compete with two such goddesses, was pleased she had settled for a soft yellow gown, ruffed and long and straight, with long pointed sleeves and a little embroidered cap of the same material that came to a point above her forehead, with a dangling large, and obviously false, pearl in the manner of Mary Queen of Scots.

All formality forgotten, they laughed and began to circle and admire each other, the men proclaiming they had not had much choice. Deveron had made off with the only outfit of elegance so they had to settle for uniforms since the court costumes were found in too poor condition. Rushdon looked very much the captain in a red uniform he said cheerfully might have been worn in any of the wars in America, he wasn't up on the old styles and insignia; and Gifford and Fernando had settled for green and brown. Lord Deveron, looking a little sheepish and therefore endearing, was magnificent in a blue and white outfit with puffed breeches and sleeves and tight doublet, lace at the throat and a little blue cape swinging from his shoulders, and a blue hat with a bedraggled white ostrich feather.

"Don't know what it is," he said apologetically, "Stuart, probably, but I never had a chance to wear anything like it—I thought as the host I might indulge myself, but . . ."

"You did quite right," Thea reassured him gaily. "It is most becoming and the host has a duty to look his best." She wished one of the famous painters could put down on canvas that engaging figure now so enhanced by the costume. To his evident relief, her praise was repeated by Mrs. Farraby and Lord Ledgefield. The two explained they had consulted but decided they were beyond the age of dressing up, and the comfort of their own clothes was vastly preferred to the most beautiful of costumes of bygone days. The sherry was being passed and the circle not yet broken when Mrs. Farraby gave a little shriek. "But who is this?"

A figure that seemed abnormally tall was walking easily

toward them from the steps. Brown leather trousers were tucked in the wide tops of boots, a long sleeveless jacket of leather lay over a plain white shirt. A leather band across the chest diagonally, descending to the belt, held a sword on the left side. The hat, without feathers, was wide-brimmed and caught up on one side with a gold buckle. The jacket and trousers and boots were worn and rubbed. Here was obviously a very capable fighting man. He stopped, smiled a little crookedly and reached for a sherry.

"Bourne!" cried Thea.

"But . . . who?" asked Rushdon.

Bourne tossed back the sherry. "The last man who wore this outfit was a young lieutenant of cavalry, and aide to Rupert—Rupert of the Rhine, they called him— nigh a genius and general of the cavalry of his cousin Charles the First. He'd have made a better king of England than any of the Stuarts. The lad who wore this was wounded at Marston Moor and brought home by his best friend to die." He stopped and reached for another sherry. There was a pause for a moment until Rushdon said, "By Jove. And I wager he looked like you." At which Bourne looked as embarrassed as Deveron had been.

Why, he's romantic, thought Thea, and he said he wasn't. I should have known. Impulsively she crossed to him and held out her hand. "Welcome, Lieutenant. You honor us."

"Thank you." His hand closed over hers. She knew her eyes were smiling warmly and her smile wide and did not care, as he gave her a searching look and bent to kiss her fingers.

As if a party of statues was released from a spell, all began to talk and move, the men quite shamelessly examining each other's costumes until Costanza, half laughing, half imperious, called to them to at least speak to the ladies. Shamefacedly they returned to their duties as gallants and were rallied for their preoccupation with each other.

Wisely, Thea felt, the dinner was not overburdened with many dishes, featuring trout, a fricandeau of veal with vegetable pudding, peas, two soups, larded sweetbreads, strawberries doused in wine and various creams and cakes, none of it beyond the prowess of the kitchen, and all served neatly and devoured completely. In the candlelight of the cool, stately room the group around the table was magnificent, and felt it, for the laughter and gaiety never ceased.

"It's the fancy dress," observed Bourne on Thea's left. "Makes everyone feel a different person."

"Quite true," approved Lord Ledgefield opposite, "and an excellent thing, too, to be free of one's own self on occasion. Should happen more often."

"But there is no telling where that freedom would lead," Thea twinkled. "Gentlemen, now, can change their character with their country and city, morning and evening dress, and must be accustomed to their own variety. But ladies remain much the same these dull days. If we should really don strange garments and acquire other characters, there is no telling into what adventure we might be led."

"Eh?" Both men gave her a startled look. Lord Ledgefield began to laugh. "Very clever, Miss Minturn. Gives one ideas . . ." For a flash Bourne's gaze was intent, and Thea wished she knew what he was thinking, then he chuckled and looked around the table. "Oh, we all feel fine fellows tonight, and I'll wager every lady feels she's her five favorite heroines rolled into one."

"You're all certainly enjoying yourselves," nodded Lord Ledgefield. "Almost makes me wish I were young again. But then, Susan and I agreed we are content to have had our youth when we did and now our present."

"I hope I shall have your good sense, when needed," Thea told him seriously.

He looked at her briefly from under bushy gray eyebrows. "'You will, my dear, but there—Susan's trying to catch your eye." Thea caught it and rose and carried off the ladies to the large saloon.

Over coffee Costanza pointed out that the room was quite large enough for dancing and even had a spinet and was delighted when Mrs. Farraby allowed she could make sounds like a waltz and would be happy to do so if nothing more was required of her. Footmen were summoned to move back furniture and rugs and open the windows more widely. It was Captain Rushdon who bowed before Thea at the first moment, and she was grateful to him since Bourne had headed quickly for Costanza, and Cordelia had turned expectantly to Deveron. The dances were short and more lively than customary and allowed frequent changes of partners.

There was a heightened air almost of expectation in the long room as if each person felt a new personality had been added with the costumes and that something new was sure to happen. Thea regretted she could not think of some mad game to meet the exuberance and remembered the hide-and-seek at Wilton. If only they were not so far from High Wyfells, they could have worked off their energy among the figures in the yew garden and suited the place to perfection. They were ready for anything, and she was about to ask Lord Ledgefield for suggestions for the music had stopped and they had moved toward the center of the room.

Before she could the portly butler paced into the room. "My lord," he intoned, "Miss Ariel Kempton begs your permission to call."

"Of course." Deveron stepped forward. "Who . . . ? Where is she?"

"Here, my lord," fluted a light sweet voice, and a slight figure in a white ruffed gown moved composedly into the room. Thea blinked. Pale gold hair stood as an oreole behind a long pale face with eyes of light blue. She looked familiar, but Thea was sure she had never seen the girl. She came to Deveron, bowed a little, and turned to Thea and dipped a curtsey. "You must be Miss Minturn," she lilted. "So kind of you to permit me to join you."

"Pleasure," Deveron told her smoothly. "Another lady for the dancing is most welcome."

The white face looked around the room composedly. "And this one I hope particularly. I had thought to defer my visit until tomorrow, but then I heard you were having a costume ball. By chance the gown I had made from the portrait was with me. I could not resist the impulse to join you in the home of my ancestors and as a descendant of Lucy Freane and Sir Richard. No doubt you have noticed the resemblance. I have come to the aid of my family. I will find the Zamora emeralds for you."

"What?" demanded Deveron.

"How kind," said Thea at the same moment and felt the others move closer.

"Why, yes." The sweet smile held a touch of condescension. "I was only lately apprised of the will of Lord Stanford and its conditions. And, just recently, that there is a noble lady here for the same purpose. In her own way, she is a witch. It is my belief she will fail, but I felt it my duty to make sure the emeralds remain in the family, they belong to us. Since I have the means to find them I have come to the aid of my cousins. Also, I cannot deny a selfish motive which you must perceive," she lowered her eyes and her voice became a little apologetic, "since they may possibly one day be mine."

"Oh, I say," protested Mr. Gifford feebly.

"I only said possibly," she pointed out a little quickly, "and all things are possible. Anything may happen." The eyes were still lowered. "It is a feeling I have that fate, chance, what you will, will bring them to me."

Involuntarily Thea glanced at Deveron and met his

somewhat startled look. Then, with an air that would have done credit to Mr. Brummell, Deveron stepped to the girl and offered his arm. "But first, ma'am, you must permit me to make you acquainted with our company." He conducted her to Mrs. Farraby, to whom a deferential curtsey was made, then around to the others. Thea could feel the atmosphere of the room settling down from anticipation to curiosity. At the end, Deveron asked politely, "Do you care to find the emeralds now?"

No one had moved except Costanza whose foot was tapping the floor. She opened her mouth, but her brother laid a hand on her arm and she closed it.

Again Mr. Gifford entered the silence. "I say," he began, examining the newcomer with interest. "Pretty name, Ariel. Suits you. But how do we know you are the next cousin?"

"Oh, I knew I would forget." She trilled a little laugh. "I have brought a note from Mr. Tillingborne." From a white crocheted bag she produced a piece of paper and handed it to Deveron who gave it a glance and put it in Thea's hand. She was glad of the excuse to leave the circle for the nearest candelabra as the girl added, "It was only proper to bring that, though you would have guessed."

During the murmur that followed, Thea saw that the note said the bearer had called to inform him she was Anne Kempton, the next heir to Miss Minturn under the will, and was on her way to call at Ardsley Hall.

"How guessed?" Lord Bourne asked lazily as Thea rejoined the group. Mrs. Farraby and Lord Ledgefield were at ease on a sofa but well within earshot, and Costanza's toe was still tapping.

"Why, my resemblance to our ancestress, of course." Miss Kempton was surprised at the question. "You have seen the portrait. I am very like her, even at such a long remove."

"How surprising!" said Cordelia faintly.

"Indeed," Miss Kempton agreed, "but that is my good fortune."

We are all so surprised, Thea thought, we are behaving like a bunch of lumpkins. "Mr. Tillingbourne's note gives the name Anne," she said, "but you said . . . ?"

"Ariel." There came the trill. "Anne is my given name, but ever since I was small I have been called Ariel as appropriate."

"Do you wish to find the emeralds now?" Deveron asked again courteously. "May we be of assistance?"

"Oh, no." A little restraint crept into the light voice. "That will take time, for I do not know where I will find them."

"But," began Costanza hotly, "wherever they are, they are ours."

Pale eyebrows rose. "We will settle everything most amicably, Condesa, I am convinced. Right, after all, is right." The matter was dismissed.

Thea felt it her duty to act the hostess and went to the girl. "Since it will take time to find them, you will surely wish to stay in the Hall. We will, of course, be most happy to have you as our guest. You will prefer to be in the older portion where the ladies are staying. May I send for your boxes?"

Miss Kempton's smile was as wide as the rather small mouth permitted. "Dear Miss Minturn, cousin. I was sure of your hospitality, so I brought my boxes with me. They are even now in the other house, and Mrs. Brewton promised me she would have a room ready when I returned. I knew, you see, that you would say just those words. But then I often do know things in advance."

"Horse races?" Mr. Gifford asked eagerly.

The smile turned forgiving. "No, sir. That is too mundane. It is in matters of the family, and the spirit, that I sometimes have prescience."

Thea judged from Mr. Gifford's expression that he

would need to have the words explained to him sometime but hoped he would not be discouraged from asking whatever came into his head. She took up her own part. "You did not come alone? Your abigail?"

"My cousin, on my father's side, not ours, and his wife brought me from Scarborough. We spent the night at an inn near Dylson so I could call upon Mr. Tillingbourne this morning and then came on to the Rose and Crown. In fact, dear cousin," and the trill came again, "I knew so well how kind you would be that I sent my cousin back immediately to the inn."

Thea remembered what Bourne had told her about the upstairs maid and her aunt at that inn. She would have liked to countermand her invitation and send word to Mrs. Brewton to remove the new boxes. But she smiled a little and glanced at Deveron. "My lord, do you not think the tea table is in order now? Would you ring?"

The footmen were again summoned to replace chairs and rugs and people began to move around, though inclined to circle the newcomer a little warily. Thea stayed firmly beside her until the room was arranged and chairs could be occupied. The feeling of the room was changed; it had been so gay and now there was a sense of unease. All wished to ask questions, and no one felt it fitting to quiz Miss Kempton on any subject.

But Mr. Gifford carried her tea cup and drew up a chair. "Jolly interesting what you have to say, Miss Kempton, about knowing things, all that. We had a housemaid once who said she was the seventh daughter of the seventh daughter and could read tea leaves, minds, too. But my mother let her go before I could find out. Always been sorry."

"It is quite possible the maid could do that." The light voice turned a little solemn. "We all have powers of which we are unaware."

That so startled Mr. Gifford he turned silent. Bourne

remarked, a little loudly, "We may have them but they never come when needed. How do you make yours work, Miss Kempton?"

She shook a playful finger at him. "You should not ask, my lord. It is different for all, for what we have is born in us."

Mr. Gifford had recovered. "But how are you going to find the emeralds?"

Again the playful finger moved. "You will see when the time comes."

"Bah," said Costanza rather violently from the other side of the table. "You mean the spirit of your—your ancestress, that whey-faced creature, will come and tell you? I tell you she will not. If my ancestress, a creature of fire and intelligence, could not tell me, that wraith will be no help to you."

Someone moved a candelabra and the hair became a nimbus above the gentle smile. "Perhaps you and she are not in tune, Condesa. Or perhaps she does not know where our Sir Richard hid them for she was gone at that time. One of the reasons I feel you will fail. You have a certain power, I am aware, but our powers do not always work with our desires. But since there is, again, the remote possibility you might succeed, I have come to the rescue of the family. The emeralds must remain with us." There could be no doubt she would do her utmost to see they did.

As Costanza snorted, Bourne brought his cup to Thea for more tea. "I'm not going off to the wars, in spite of my uniform," he murmured, his eyes dancing. "The wars here will be more entertaining. But watch out you don't get caught in between opposing forces. Often happens to innocents, you know. Did I compliment you on your choice of gowns? I should have. It is most becoming, would appeal to the chivalry in any man." He looked more amused at her surprise, gave her a little bow, and sauntered away. Though pleased at his compliment, Thea, rather forlornly, would have liked to ask him what innocents could do when they were caught between opposing forces.

She waited until all had completed the refreshments and then rose. "My lord," she said formally to Deveron, "we thank you for a delightful dinner and evening. But we are weary from all that has been done today so we must make our adieux." She was relieved the others rose without hesitation and left them to make their farewells while she made a point of picking up Miss Kempton and guiding her to the other house and up to the room Mrs. Brewton had indeed prepared. She had no desire to linger, nor did the girl invite her, and went to her own room and closed the door. That would discourage any visitor anxious to discuss—anything. She did not wish to waste hours in fruitless speculation.

Eleven

FOR A number of minutes she lay watching through the window the solitary cloud hang motionless in the blue sky and decided she would not get up for breakfast. Ardsley and its guests could entertain themselves. If an interesting war did develop as Bourne predicted, she would draw the curtains, lock her door, and go into a fit of strong hysterics. The prospect held certain attractions for then she would be absent when this Ariel and Costanza came to hair-pulling. Would Cordelia, like the Roman matron she so resembled (or was it the Sabine women) throw herself between them? Which of the ladies would attract the stronger cohorts to her defense? Cousin Susan would judge the contest, unless, of course, it was decided by the emeralds themselves. At that thought she sat up. Even if she didn't want them, no one was going off with her share. Would Deveron divide his half between the blonde and the brunette? Would he divide himself? No, in spite of tuggings at the leash, Cordelia still seemed to have him fast, but then, perhaps she didn't. Bourne was paying particular attention to his friend from South America. It was her duty, she told herself, to put in an appearance even if she felt too frail to lift a finger. Once up, to her annoyance, she found she was filled with anticipation and rang for her morning chocolate.

What a treasure Cousin Susan was, Thea thought as she entered the dining room, the morning room having proved too small because of the gentlemen. Mrs. Farraby was at the coffee looking, as always, calm, gently entertained, and capable. No wonder Lord Ledgefield was hovering. . . . Besides, she had wit, which she did not often use but which would appeal to any man of intelligence. The three young ladies in morning frocks of pastel shades were enjoying the breakfast and giving every air of utmost amiability. As she entered, Ariel jumped up and came to make a dip to Thea. "Dear cousin, you are so good to me. Such a comfortable room and bed. I vow I shall never wish to leave."

"I am pleased you slept well," Thea managed. That dip was to appeal to her finer sensibilities, but it failed, and she thought the last sentence in dubious taste, all things considered. In the daylight Ariel's hair was still a nimbus, and Thea decided it must be the wiry type that was stiff when short. The girl did have the high forehead and long upper lip of the portrait. . . .

Ariel sped back to her chair. "I was telling how I came to see the portrait of our ancestress. My mother brought me with her to solicit the patronage of Lord Stanford in furthering the career of my brother, Jack, in the navy. His lordship was from home, but in view of the relationship Brewton conducted us to the portrait gallery so I might see my ancestors. My mother was struck immediately by my resemblance to the Lady Stanford. The other house was closed. Nor did I see it, or his lordship, when I came a few years ago to ask his guidance about my future."

Since no comment was forthcoming Thea asked, "And Jack?"

"Killed in the Battle of the Nile," Ariel said sadly, "but
. . ."

"When I first saw the portrait of Isabella Maria,"
Costanza broke in, "it was at the palace of my uncle the
Duque in Madrid. There as a small child, you understand, on a visit, I was led into the vast state room, hung
with tapestries, a huge portrait of our emperor over the
fireplace, and only three other portraits on the walls. Two
footmen help up large tapers, and there was Isabella
Maria, beautiful, flashing, so much a better likeness than
that trifle upstairs, looking at me. My grandmother told
me 'She is saying, Costanza, it is you who will return the
emeralds to our house.' And I then vowed I would."

"Naturally. But she did get home." Kindness was in
each of Ariel's syllables. "I am convinced all our family
has always been happy that she was rescued and in such
a gallant fashion."

"The emeralds should have gone with her." Costanza's
voice rose a little.

"Well, I always thought that largely a matter of the
right of possession," said Ariel as if trying to put it in
a judicious light. Fortunately before Costanza could
gather herself to rout that attitude, Deveron led in his
guests prepared for a second breakfast. "Beautiful day,"
he announced.

"Oh, it is," cooed Ariel. "I was up, so early, and went
out to walk in the dew on the lovely grass. The dew, the
new sun, the flowers, birds, all so uplifting."

"By Jove," said Mr. Gifford with admiration. "Never
tried early hours myself, but no doubt you're right,
ma'am," and beamed in return at her smile.

"Inspiration, too?" Deveron inquired, head tilted on
one side. "You wish to start now retrieving the emeralds?"

A movement caught Thea's eye. Costanza, though her
smile was bland, was gazing at her with anxious entreaty.

"I'm sure Miss Kempton is weary from her long journey," Thea interposed before the idea could be acclaimed. "She undoubtedly wishes to recoup her strength and to become acquainted with Ardsley Hall." She smiled gently at the girl and doubted that she was as frail as she made herself appear. "Particularly since it may one day be hers."

"By Jove, yes," Mr. Gifford ejaculated. "Forgot that. Why . . ."

"But when I do find the emeralds, then that condition is fulfilled, and Miss Minturn and Lord Deveron will be in possession," she pointed out a little loudly. "I am here for the sake of the family—that is all, you must understand."

"Miss Minturn is right," Deveron agreed. "You need time . . ."

"No," Miss Kempton told him with all seriousness. "Instantly I could go to work. But I confess I would so enjoy a day exploring the house, the beautiful gardens, the home of my ancestors."

"Ours," corrected Thea. "Then of course you may have the day. Wander around alone or with what company you wish."

"I do not wish to interfere with anyone. And please call me Ariel. I am so accustomed to it I hardly respond to the other."

"As you wish. So we will all occupy ourselves today with whatever is most appealing." Thea felt she must get the reins back in her own hands. "And now," she proclaimed, "we will have hot coffee, please, Brewton, and whatever remains from that delicious breakfast."

While the remains were being appreciated, Brewton brought Thea a note. She had to knock on the table to make herself heard. The faces turned toward her like a ring of pansies. "Lord Bourne has sent to invite us to tea at High Wyfells tomorrow. Shall I accept for us?" She had every intention of accepting, but had decided to make another show of catering to their wishes, and was pleased at the enthusiasm of their acceptance.

After a demure show of protests, Ariel decided she would prefer above all to walk about the older house. Mr. Gifford gallantly asserted he would go with her for he now knew the house so well he could guard her against the unexpected turns of the halls and twists of the older stairs. Fernando said he would accompany them before Mr. Gifford could formulate any objection. Thea then announced there would be a cold luncheon and all were expected for dinner, but not in costume, and left the room ahead of the others.

In the hall Deveron caught up with her and motioned to the estate office, and when she followed him in, he closed the door. "What think you of this Kempton girl, Thea?" he asked seriously.

She leaned against the side of the flat desk and looked at him uncertainly. "I do not know. She is convincing in her own way but she says so little of moment about herself, her background. We must permit her to use whatever means she has to find the emeralds."

"Of course." He gestured impatiently and crossed to look out the window. "Convenient room, this, wish I had one such." He came back and sat on the arm of the chair. "I would not give the girl credence except that she said she came to make sure the emeralds stay in the family since she feels they may some day come to her."

"That is a most convincing motive," Thea agreed. "She must have confidence in her success or she would not venture here. In fact," she added thoughtfully, "she almost acts as if she were ready to take over Ardsley at any moment."

"Yes, I have felt that. But," he smiled reassuringly, "you and I are still very much in possession and she may be enacting something of which she has long dreamed."

"A way girls have, particularly if they are ambitious

and have heard tales of family wealth they do not share." She threw out her hands. "No matter what lies behind her, we must afford her every courtesy. But I do hope she may not succeed, for then we would have a most distressing encounter between her and Costanza, and I do not know how we could resolve it."

"I shudder at the thought." He stood up. "But let us not concern ourselves with that now, for it may not happen. In fact, I do not believe she will succeed. I just wanted to make sure you felt the same uncertainty about her that I do, and I agree we must behave as if we believed her, at least until tomorrow morning."

He stopped on his way to the door to look at her. "You are really an unusual girl, Thea, and I must confess to feelings of increasing friendliness and gratitude, for I do not know how I would get on in this situation without you." He opened the door for her and instead of bowing patted her shoulder. "Again, I am trusting your good sense," he said softly.

Pondering his words and her own feelings, Thea mounted to her room but before she could close her door, Costanza had rushed in and thrown her arms around her. "You are my true friend, Thea. I could say nothing, but I knew I could trust you." Thea found herself being kissed on both cheeks. "You have given me this day. I will disappear. Do not let anyone seek me." She dropped her arms and whirled. "And that statue, as I call her, she can have Deveron all day for all the good it will do her." There was a snap of fingers and Costanza was gone.

When Thea came downstairs she found Captain Rushdon in the library. His slow smile and large solid figure were reassuring after Costanza. The girl had aroused Thea's concern for she seemed to be taking her quest more and more seriously.

"Nice room, this." The Captain waved a hand around. "Cheerful, with all the red, and it doesn't put one off by being formal. I like old houses and have tried to learn a little about them, when I could." He walked to the window. "Nice day. Not too warm. Could you bear my company for a while? I am hoping you might care for a ride. If I'm not too bold, we could get quite away from Ardsley for a while, though I admit that's hardly proper."

"It sounds proper and delightful to me," Thea told him gaily. "Order up the horses, and I'll be right down."

Captain Rushdon, as always, was a comfortable companion. When asked of his experiences, he disallowed their importance and spoke of the people and lands where he had soldiered. When they spoke of London, he was amusing and never malicious. When they came to the guests, he allowed they were unusual and then laughed.

"No, I'm not being namby-pamby, Miss Minturn, and I do not always see the best of everyone, or even redeeming features. But people interest me, and I always feel if one knew more of them, one could understand more about them, but then that would apply to me also, and I am not sure I should care for that." He chuckled. "It is a strange collection here and one wonders what will happen which, after all, is the best part of life—anticipation. But come, I know the lanes a little, and there is a hedgerow tavern where they'll bring us out tankards of a very fair ale, if you care for it." And Thea thought of him again as a man of sensibility, he did not scold or scorn, like some others, or arouse any emotions, so he was restful.

They were ambling down a lane so sunken between hedgerows of hawthorn and wild cherry that the effect was of a green tunnel dappled with the gold of sunlight. The small ale had been refreshing and Thea felt at peace with the world. But Captain Rushdon began to speak in a more serious voice. "I only met Lord Stanford once, he was not an intimate of my uncle. He was one of those eccentrics in whom we English take pride while being glad we are not as they, and who are such a nuisance to their friends and our consuls in foreign lands. For example, there is his infamous will. I would like to say, Miss Minturn, that I have admired the calm manner in which you have handled this delicate situation. What course you may decide to pursue, or what may be forced upon you, cannot be anticipated, but I would like you to know I have developed feelings for you warmer than respect. I am not my uncle's heir, merely his preferred nephew. My estate in Herefordshire is small. If you should decide to marry, and if you could bring yourself to do so, I beg you will give me the privilege of offering for your hand. In fact," he went on with a rush, "if I may be permitted, I am now."

Thea reined in and gazed at him with open surprise. "Captain Rushdon! I—I am overcome. You do me great honor. But I do not know. . ."

He leaned toward her and put one hand over hers. "Of course you do not. That I would not expect. I have been precipitate. You have had, will have, other offers. But I felt I must not wait longer to tell you of the deep affection I feel for you and my desire to make your whole life happy. Do not say more now. You cannot. It is enough for me that I have told you how matters stand with me. I must add, though I trust it is not necessary, that it is not the possibility of the possession of half of Ardsley Hall that has prompted me. I vastly prefer my own small place. But your wishes would always be paramount with me."

He looked deeply into her face and the hard soldier's eyes were replaced by an appealing warmth. He pressed her hand and removed his. "Say nothing now, but remember. I will not mention this again." He straightened. "I am no hand at declaring myself, Miss Minturn, for I have never before. Forgive my awkwardness, but I pray you will remember my devotion. Now, would you care to canter?"

For a few moments Thea knew she was thrown into confusion. This she had never expected. He had spoken in all sincerity. It was true she might find herself in need of a husband, but, as with Mr. Salton, it would be infamous to accept his offer for her benefit alone. But she would always hold him in gratitude.

During luncheon Thea kept wondering what she could suggest to entertain these people for the evening and keep Costanza and Ariel apart. She was saved from the desperate solution of proclaiming a causerie by a note from Mrs. Chelworth. She begged that Miss Minturn and her guests would forgo all formality and favor their home, The Elms, for a small affair, long planned for friends, with just cards, games, supper. She had thought it only fitting to offer some hospitality. Since they kept country hours, the affair would not bring undue fatigue. Thea did not pause to inquire whether the others were willing, for she was sure they would be as pleased as she at the prospect of a diversion, and accepted with near enthusiasm.

Gratefully she retired to her room but paused. Costanza had not been in the dining room. No one had spoken of her. What could the girl have been doing these hours? If she were asleep she could remain, but her room was empty. It was unlikely she would go into the gardens in midday. Slowly Thea went down again and mounted the turning stairs of the tower to the third floor.

On the stone bench by the center window Costanza was huddled, her face in her hands, long shudders shaking her body. No emeralds then, thought Thea—the poor girl—and hurried across to kneel on the floor and put her arms around the quivering figure. "My dear," she whispered. "Don't weep so. What is the matter?"

The dark head shook, then huge eyes in a white face

lifted to hers. "No. I must be alone. To face my shame."

"Nonsense" was the first word to come to Thea, but that would not do. She rose and sat on the bench and put her arm around the shoulders. "There now. There is no shame. You are distraught." The head lifted and Thea pulled it down on her shoulder. "There," she soothed again. "Nothing is worth all these tears."

A white hand reached to clutch Thea's. "Yes. You I would like to tell. You only . . . and Fernando."

"There is no need to tell me," began Thea.

"I wish. So you will understand. It was my pride, the pride of all the Villamayos, that led me into this. But I was so sure . . ." She paused and shuddered and sat up straight. "I must compose myself to speak clearly. It is this way. I have been sure for always, since I was a little girl, that I would someday find the Zamora emeralds. I did not know how, but when the Englishman fell into our doorway I knew the way would open. Always I have had a little of what is called foreknowledge, the sureness sometimes of what is going to happen, when people would arrive, what some would say. It was accepted, but most of all because of one night."

Her hands lay quiet in her lap, and she was looking fixedly at the far side of the room. "We were on our way to the *estancia* in the hills to spend the warm months. It was late spring. We were camped by a shallow river. I went to sleep and then suddenly I saw Inez, my ama, my nurse for ten years until she went back to her mountains to die. She was an Aymara, an Inca Pura, she held, and never told us her real name. We loved each other, oh, so dearly. I wept for nights after she left. This night by the river she appeared before me, wringing her hands and pointing to the mountains and moaning '*agua, agua,*' and made her arms swoop down. I knew she was telling me there had been rains high in the mountains and the snows had melted and the waters were coming. She vanished. I ran to my father and by the grace of the Virgin he believed me, and we broke our camp and drove the horses and wagons as far as we could from the river. By dawn a great torrent was rushing down and covering where we had been."

She stopped again and looked appealingly at Thea. "That is enough to set one up a little, is it not? No one forgot it. My grandmother had told me how much I looked like Isabella Maria and that it would be I who would bring back the emeralds to the family. One hears that from someone convinced, and one becomes convinced. And so I believed if I could come here and wait, Isabella would speak to me and show me the treasure as Inez had appeared to save our lives. Twice I have waited, so long, my mind held so empty, but nothing. And now my pride is gone and I am ashamed." The head went down again.

Thea patted her shoulder. The girl would go into hysterics if she were not careful. "But you should not think of your pride, my dear," she began carefully. "It is not your fault you have not found those stones. Perhaps it is that Isabella could not tell you. And," inspiration came, "it may be that it is because this search is for selfish reasons, for . . . for the pride of the family. Inez appeared to you for unselfish reasons, to save you because she loved you so greatly." That sounded pretty thin to her, but Costanza looked up and her eyes were brighter.

"You are right. It is a lesson to me, to the family, that we should not be so worldly, think so much of wealth and riches. Oh, dear Thea, you have shown me that I, we, were wrong. I will be resigned never to see the emeralds. I will convince my family. Unless," she added, "that white-faced *puta maldita* finds them, and then I will tear them from her."

"She won't," Thea told her confidently. "Now, you must stop crying. We are going to a party tonight, and you must lie down and I will bring a cold compress for your eyes."

"Costanza," came a low call. "You are there? I have looked for you." Fernando rushed to the bench, knelt and held out his arms. "My dear sister, it is all right."

She leaned forward to kiss him. "I will be so. Our dear Thea found me. She has understood, has showed me, but, oh, I am so glad to see you."

Thea rose and crept away and sought a cold compress for her own eyes and a peaceful hour in her own room.

The company at The Elms, a comfortable manor house some four miles to the west, consisted of four older couples and ten young people whose faces were vaguely familiar. Thea introduced Ariel as her cousin, which aroused only a little interest. The elders retired to whist in the card room. There was a little stiffness at first, there was no room for dancing, but when a game of Speculation was proposed all moved to the dining room and, in the explanation of the game and the rules to the willing but rather bewildered Spaniards, the stiffness vanished. Thea was rather surprised at first at the spirit with which Deveron entered the game and the unbending of Cordelia, but then realized they were country raised and knew the game from their youth. She was laughing and looking for a chair when Fernando touched her arm and begged her to walk with him for a few minutes on the front terrace. She liked, but did not know at all, this quiet young man and went willingly.

"I wish to thank you, Thea, for what you have done for my sister, for the sustaining strength of your concern," he began immediately. "She told me what you said. I wish to explain a little."

She put up a hand. "That is not necessary. Your sister has suffered a grievous disappointment. Her emotion is understandable."

"I am grateful for your perception. She has always done as she wished because of her beauty and intelligence —and her spirit and determination. This search for the family emeralds was planted in her, unfortunately, by our grandmother, and it is but natural it should appeal to a romantic girl. In part, I am convinced, that has been behind her refusal to marry. She was so confident. . . . Our father can never withstand her pleas, her desires. Then came an opportunity—Costanza felt she must seize it. I love her dearly, and so does my affianced wife who waits for me at home. It was agreed I should come with her, to care for her, and it has been unexpectedly delightful. Now, I believe, she will see more and more, thanks to the wisdom of your words, that her quest was not intended to succeed, indeed should not. Very gladly I will take her home and endeavor to make sure of her future happiness. And it is thanks to you and to Bourne that our memories of this time in England will be among our most happy." He made a formal little bow.

She put her hand on his arm. "I must thank you for revealing all this, and I am sure you are right in all respects. I have become fond of your sister, and I wish her all happiness. If there is ever aught I can do to assist you in that, pray tell me."

He raised her hand to his lips. "I will," he said simply. "Again I thank you."

When they returned, they found the game had become hilarious and so complicated that it lasted until the supper was served. Thea's gratitude for the invitation when she said farewell to Mrs. Chelworth was heartfelt, for the game had kept all from thinking about anything else.

The entire party descended at the gatehouse and paused to admire a somewhat misshapen moon. "Beautiful night," ejaculated Mr. Gifford. "Not yet midnight. Plenty of time, Ariel, now, for you to unearth those stones."

"Oh, no." Ariel's emphatic words practically echoed

from the walls. "It is not that I could not. But I confess I am weary. The day has been enchanting, but so full. Would not tomorrow morning be more pleasing to us all? After breakfast?"

The murmurs were indistinguishable, but she took them as agreement and almost went into the house ahead of Thea, but was foiled by Thea's shoulder.

Twelve

EVIDENTLY MR. GIFFORD had waked with the same notion with which he had gone to sleep, for he was hurrying all to finish before the serving dishes were half empty. "Here now. We mustn't dawdle. Miss Kempton is about to demonstrate her gift."

"No, no," she protested. "I will only be doing my duty. I can assure you, cousins, that nothing is buried in the gardens. I have been over them."

"A relief," Deveron said smoothly. "Walker would not permit us to take up any turf even if the jewels of Solomon were underneath. Then where?"

Ariel sat up straight. "It is agreed, by all, I have heard," she began didactically, "that the hiding place must be in this the older house. Since all houses are subject to alteration, a hiding place should be chosen some place that is not likely to be touched. So it would seem we must confine our search to the older rooms. I rule out the cellar because it would have been difficult for one man to construct there a hiding place."

"Good, ho," approved Mr. Gifford. "Don't care for cellars."

"Also the attics," went on Ariel. "They are open and not of sufficiently substantial construction."

"Thought it all out, she has." Mr. Gifford shook his head admiringly. "Attics too hot, anyway."

"So," Ariel rose gracefully, "we will begin with one obvious room, the portrait gallery. I will meet you there in ten minutes."

Amid an impressed silence she left the dining room. Thea was sure she wished she could have floated.

Sunlight was pouring into the Long Gallery bringing a shine to the dark panels and a glow to the portraits. Thea had just begun to examine the oldest when Ariel appeared in the far doorway. In one hand she held a forked stick.

She was obviously delighted by their surprise. "See," she held up the stick, "this is my guide." It was about a foot and a half high, one end forming a V so the whole was in the shape of a Y. It was smooth, pale tan in color, and quite unremarkable. "You may feel it," she said graciously and held it out to Deveron who ran a finger over one prong and placed it in Gifford's hand. "It is quite stiff, is it not," Ariel went on complacently. "Lord Bourne, seize the prongs and you will discover it is firm and not to be moved." Costanza, eying it as if it were a snake, refused to touch it, at which Ariel laughed delightedly. "It is quite harmless. It will perform for no one but me. You need have no fears." Thea felt the smoothness of the sturdy wood and returned it.

"It is wild birch, though there are several woods that may be used, but of course none of the evergreens for they do not have the right properties," Ariel informed them. "If you will retreat to the windows I will begin."

As they backed away she walked to the corner of the room by the door, faced the opposite wall, and began to walk slowly down the floorboard, holding the stick upright by a prong in each hand. The stem remained straight up. She reached the far fireplace, paced slowly around

the hearth and went back to the opposite wall. Once
more she went up and down and then shook her head.
"There is nothing in this room."

"What is that thing?" demanded Mr. Gifford loudly.

Ariel paused in the full light from a window and gave
him a happy smile. "It is my dowsing rod. It will find
things that cannot be found by any other method. It is
most used for finding water, and in Lincolnshire I have
a name for being pleasantly successful at that. Of course
I do not charge for finding water for a farm, that is sharing my gift as one should. But it can find metals, lost
objects—not invariably, of course, that would be too
much—but frequently enough so that my services are
sought. As I have said, I brought it here of my own will.
But we are wasting time here. The bedrooms are possibilities, but the ground floor is the most likely."

Before Thea could nod, she was gliding toward the
door, went down to the state bedroom, and walked in,
holding her rod.

"Rugs?" asked Thea faintly.

"They do not matter. Nothing can matter." She walked
through the other rooms and reached what had once been
a schoolroom, for it held three plain desks and chairs and
a rocker. Glancing around, she went to the corner window and back to the fireplace and was about to move
away when the upright rod gave a faint quiver. She
halted, took a step toward the corner of the hearth and
the rod quivered again, bent forward a few inches, and
stayed there.

"Why did you do that?" Deveron asked.

"*I* did not do it. It is the rod. There is something here,
not much, but shall we see?" She stayed posed above a
corner board until Deveron returned with a chisel and
mallet, looking inquiringly at Thea, and at her nod in-
serted the blade, tappd and began to pry up.

Beneath the board was a hollow. Deveron lifted out a

small dagger with a broken point, five dull copper coins, and three blackened ones that showed silver at one edge.

"Roman coins, I'll wager," said Bourne softly. "Dagger much later. Some boy found and hid them. Miss Kempton, I bow."

"But that is nothing," Ariel proclaimed as they crowded to see the find. As she moved away the rod straightened. They all followed her very willingly to the hall, the stairs, the gatehouse which she dismissed with a wave of a hand and a " . . . stones too heavy for one man" to Deveron, and went into the library. As always, with the red of the leather chairs, draperies, rug, decorations and uniforms in two portraits, the room was brightly cheerful. "Go and stay by the windows," she directed. Obediently they found places.

As before, she went to the far corner and began to cross the floor toward the windows and return. The fourth return took her near the fireplace. As she advanced the rod quivered, at the next step it was slowly waving. She stepped on the corner block of marble of the hearth, and the rod gave a leap and pointed straight down.

"Gad!" ejaculated Mr. Gifford and started forward.

Ariel shook her head. She moved away and the rod straightened. She walked around the hearth and across it. Only at the corner slab did the rod plunge downward. She stood still, eyes closed a moment, shook herself, and turned to the room. "It is here," she said simply. Thea felt her smile of triumph was excessively condescending, but perhaps it was justified.

"Couldn't anyone do that?" Mr. Gifford demanded suspiciously.

"Try it, all of you," Ariel laughed and held out the rod.

Eagerly he snatched it. Holding the forked stick upright, a hand on either prong of the Y, he marched up and down on and beside the fireplace. The rod made no move.

"Gad," he said again and sheepishly handed it to Deveron who only tried it briefly. Fernando waved it away with "Your magic is not ours." With Bourne the upright wavered a little at the right spot but not enough to signify.

Ariel laughed again. "Lord Bourne, if you had cultivated your powers, you might have found some that surprised you."

"No, thank you, ma'am. I'm surprised enough by those I know." His tone was light. "The ladies?"

"Do try," Ariel held out the rod. Thea was tempted but shook her head with the others.

"We'll need stronger tools," Deveron said and went for them. With apologies the men took off their jackets and began to pry and wedge the piece of marble with crowbar and wooden wedges and mallet. The stone at last tilted so it could be caught by four hands and heaved to one side. Something rough and brown lay in the gap beneath where it had been.

"Thea," Deveron's hand halted above the hole, "may I lift this?"

"Of course," she gasped. "It's half yours. I—I pray it may not be a head." Cordelia gave a moan.

At the words Deveron brought out his handkerchief to cover his hand, reached into the cavity and brought out a brown leather bag. Setting handkerchief and bag on the floor he began to feel the leather gently. Suddenly it fell apart. On the brown of the leather and white of the linen lay a pile of gold coins. For a moment there was complete silence.

Bourne knelt beside Deveron, poked the coins, lifted one. "Spanish," he announced with awe. "Deveron, see, there it says 'Dei Gratia Phillipus II.' "

"Isabella Maria's ransom," shrieked Costanza.

Deveron nodded. "No one ever knew how much there was, how much he used, how much might be left."

Costanza pushed Cordelia aside and went on her knees

beside Bourne to touch the coins and began handing them to him to place in neat stacks.

"How much they were worth then I don't know," he said. "They must be worth much more now, either to dealers in old coins or for their gold content." He raised his head and looked at Ariel, her expression pleased and proud. "Miss Kempton, it is remarkable. I am overcome. So are we all."

"Yes, yes," Costanza interrupted impatiently. "But these are not the emeralds."

"No," whispered Ariel, now downcast, clasping her rod to her. "I—to say I am sorry they are not, does not express the depths of my disappointment. I was sure I would find them." There was a flash of gratification across Costanza's expressive face. "I must apologize. . . ." The voice trailed away to nothing.

"You must not be so cast down," cried Thea. "It is wonderful beyond words what you have done for Ardsley by finding this. Lord Stanford would be so pleased. Deveron and I, we are very grateful." She hurried around the group to the pile by the hearth, stooped and picked up a coin, and went to press it into one of the narrow white hands. "Would you not keep this, from me, as a souvenir?" she asked a little breathlessly.

"And from me?" Deveron followed with another.

Ariel smiled mistily. "You are so kind." Her voice broke.

"But these are not the emeralds," Costanza repeated.

"Try again and find them?" Mr. Gifford offered hopefully.

The aureoled head shook slowly. "No. I have tried everywhere possible. I am happy that I have found this much for Ardsley. But I am convinced the emeralds are gone."

Thea looked anxiously at Costanza expecting an outburst, but the girl sank back on her heels and looked complacent. "Since you, who have done such a remark-able thing, cannot discover them, then no one can and they must indeed be gone." She was quite positive about it and gave Ariel one of her brilliant smiles. "And I truly believe you are endowed with an unusual gift," she added graciously.

Deveron was frowning down at the gold. "Eighty-five pieces you say, Bourne? Can't keep that here. Must take it to a bank in town."

"Too late today. Couldn't get there before late night."

"Tomorrow, then," Deveron said decisively. "We'll start early. I'll tell Tillingbourne on the way."

"Why, yes." Honey dripped from Costanza's voice. "Since they were undoubtedly part of the ransom for Isabella Maria, my brother and I are happy to present them to you."

There was a low. "It's theirs," from Fernando which his sister ignored as she rose to her feet, a coin in her hand. "And permit me to add to your own hoard, Ariel, as a souvenir from my ancestress."

They glanced at Bourne and found his eyes dancing. "Very pretty," he said solemnly. "Your trip was not in vain, Miss Kempton."

"Oh, no," she exclaimed, "these days here, you, my new dear friends, it has been the happiest of times, except . . ."

"Most gratifying to us all you feel that way, ma'am. Deveron, where are you going to keep this treasure until you take it to town?"

Deveron frowned down at the shining coins. He looks so handsome in shirt sleeves, Thea thought with a little pang and saw that Cordelia was regarding him and then the gold with open approval. "It's safe here," he said. "We'll put it back in that hole. No one knows about it but us. It will be easy to pry up that piece of marble to-morrow. Gifford will ride up with me."

"Honor," affirmed Mr. Gifford, "never escorted gold

before. Would prefer a beautiful lady," he added gallantly with a circling bow.

The gold was restored, the marble fitted in place, and only a keen eye would see it might have been loosened.

High Wyfells was set on its own hill, which Thea had not noticed before. As a neighbor, Thea felt vicarious pride in the oaks of the driveway and then of the house. Surrounded by greensward that was edged with low box, the house was long and low, the bricks a mellow red, the rows of wide windows promised light and air and a view. It looked comfortable and appealing in a way Ardsley never could, and Bourne in country dress, standing on the white steps to greet them, simply belonged. Even before they were all dismounted, Captain Rushdon was praising the place as an Elizabethan gem and promising to quiz Bourne at the first opportunity.

"No tea, no matter how famished you may be, until you see our topiary garden," Bourne told them, and led them to the side, down the path and through the arch, and held them for their first sight.

"But how wonderful," Costanza cried, clapping her hands. "Are they real? What are they? Are there ghosts?"

"No," Bourne told her with great firmness, "we have never had ghosts at High Wyfells." He looked sternly above Thea's head. "Come enjoy our green people."

At that they separated, wandering to one figure or another, meeting and laughing and pointing to the swaying ladies, the rearing horses.

"Wish I could ride that dragon," said Mr. Gifford unexpectedly. "Only chance I'll get at a dragon."

"He couldn't carry your weight," Bourne told him quite seriously. "And he prickles. Yes, I've tried him."

Mr. Gifford shook his head sadly and moved to admire a griffon which, rearing, offered him no temptation.

All were charmed almost beyond words, and the Spaniards proclaimed they had never seen anything like it and mourned such a garden could not be constructed at their *estancia*. Cordelia so unbent that she praised the variety of the designs and good taste and demanded of Deveron if one could not be started at Ardsley and was miffed when he pointed out it took a hundred or more years and expert special gardeners to produce such a miracle.

Before they could weary of it, Bourne herded them in to tea in the Silver Room which also brought forth extravagant admiration even though it was as old-fashioned as Cordelia held. The tea was large and lavish and Bourne an easy host. Thea would have liked to see more of the house, but as Captain Rushdon's hints in that direction were lightly turned aside because there was not time, she knew it would not be becoming.

Dinner that evening was quiet. Thea was sure they were suffering from lack of anticipation and that the savor had gone out of the visit. So she was not surprised when Lord Ledgefield told her later in the saloon that he and his nephew were compelled by duty to return to London the following day, much as they deplored it. It was not long before Cordelia informed her she had promised to spend one night with her grandmother and begged the kindness of a coach the next morning, the small one would do, since Deveron would be carrying the gold to the city. "We must all return for Lady Jersey's ball," she pointed out with some animation. "This visit has been delightful, dear Thea, but now we are restored, and so much accomplished, we must not forget our obligations in town."

Thea had quite forgotten about the ball but agreed it was of the first importance, and since it was only five days ahead she began to wonder about her own remove. With a sad smile, Ariel remarked that she must go with her cousins, who were recalled to their family. Costanza was the last to tell of their departure on the morrow. And in the end all agreed on an early start.

Some liveliness with the tea table and the farewells were prolonged by praise for the hospitality of Ardsley, the marvelous feat of Ariel, and promises to meet in town.

Though she could not feel drawn to Ariel, Thea was rather troubled that she had not done her duty by the girl and drew her aside. "It has not been possible for us to talk about Ardsley and doubtless there is much you would care to know," she said, wondering after all if she had this obligation. "Would you care to return for a visit later?"

As Ariel gazed at her tears filled the blue eyes. "Cousin, you are so kind. I would greatly enjoy such a visit. If you would direct a note to me at Upper Colfax near York, it would reach me and I would come. Now I leave with the satisfaction of not having failed entirely." She seized Thea's hand and pressed it between hers. "You will always have my gratitude." She pressed again and glided away.

As Bourne took his leave he asked carelessly, "Do you remove tomorrow also? I should think you would be in need of some recovery yourself after having this menagerie on your hands."

"How can you say such?" she chided but could not resist laughing. "I had not given the matter thought. But the ball . . . I presume we will depart in a day or so."

"As I have said before, your time is running out and you should enjoy what you can while it is possible." He gave his little bow. "I count on seeing you, then, and my gratitude for having included me so faithfully in your festivities."

"Included you!" she exploded. "I could not have kept

you out if I had wished." As he raised his eyebrows she added quickly, "Not that I would so have wished, of course, for you have been most helpful on all occasions."

"So happy to be appreciated," he murmured and laughed as he left.

Perhaps is was the excitements of the day, or the coming departure of the guests, or the return to London, but Thea found that sleep came and went to an annoying degree. The moon was low and half size but with enough light to wake her again. What would Deveron do next, once the gold was in the bank? What should be done with the gold? It added to the size of the estate but it should be put to some worthy use, something quite out of the ordinary. It was safe there, in the library below her room, and would be gone by midmorning when the servants began to clean. Had any dust been left on the floor, in case someone entered early. At that she sat up. The tools! They were where they had been laid down by the fireplace. The servants might start cleaning early, and there was Nelly with her aunt at the inn who might just go to see what they had been up to all morning. The tools would tell even someone stupid.

She put on her slippers and peignoir and eased open the door, and went down the stairs, guided by the little light from the high windows of the gatehouse. In the library she halted. She knew she was not alone for she could hear someone breathing quietly. She waited for her eyes to become accustomed to the near gloom, turned a little, and saw a dark figure standing by the corner of the hearth. She must act before that other. She ran to the fireplace and seized the crowbar still leaning at the corner and swung. She felt it hit something, knew there was a moment and that she was being hit herself and was falling.

When she opened her eyes she was convinced not many minutes had passed. Her left shoulder throbbed. She raised her head and found she was lying on a rug and except for the pain in her shoulder was entirely in command of her forces. She could feel, and hear, that she was alone. She lay still a moment, then crawled to the hearth. The marble slab was in place, the little dust she could feel would not matter. Resting a moment, she crawled farther and found chisel and mallet on the hearth, crowbar leaning on the side of the fireplace. She got to her feet and carried them, one by one, to a corner, let anyone who found them think what they would. Had she imagined it all? Her shoulder testified something had hit her. She might have tripped on the rug, she told herself, but did not believe it.

Breakfast had been set for eight because of the desired early starts. Thea was a little late for she had stopped to put a cool compress on the bruise on her shoulder. She found that all her guests were packed, the matter of the coaches had been satisfactorily settled, and all on the point of departure. She might have been put out of countenance by their gay air at leaving but understood their eagerness to put one thing behind them and look forward to whatever would happen next.

As the sounds of horses and wheels faded beyond the trees, that air of emptiness which temporarily follows when guests are gone settled over the house. Without words Thea and her cousin returned to the dining room for another cup of coffee.

Mrs. Farraby suddenly began to laugh. "It was a most successful party, my love, even though now we feel a sad letdown, which will soon pass. They all enjoyed themselves, and the entertainment could not have been more varied. I vow nothing like it could have been found from John o' Groats to Land's End."

"I was sorry for Costanza," Thea mused, "though her hopes were beyond reason."

"True. But she was greatly comforted when Miss Kempton did not find the emeralds that her own disappointment will be overborne. She will return home feeling that she has made every effort, which is always gratifying. Now I think I will repair to my room and discover how my wardrobe has survived these days." She rose and looked almost shyly at Thea. "I trust further acquaintance with Lord Ledgefield helped convince you of his amiable qualities."

"Oh, indeed." It was easy for Thea to agree warmly. "He is a most likable and entertaining gentleman and added greatly to our enjoyment, ma'am," and she twinkled at her cousin, "as well as to yours."

Mrs. Farraby nodded. "Exactly so. And you must know his nephew is much like him. But I say no more. It is for you to resolve your tangle." But she leaned over and kissed Thea, which was not her custom. If she had stayed a few minutes, Thea knew she would have been tempted to pour out all the jumble of her thoughts and emotions to her wise cousin, but later was glad that had not happened.

Thirteen

THEA WAS finishing her coffee when Deveron strode into the room. "Is Bourne here yet? Are they all gone? I'm devilish late."

"No and yes to your questions. What has happened?" He was dressed for riding and carried a canvas sack. "What of Mr. Gifford?"

"That's why I'm late." Annoyance combined with amusement. "He's not up to riding. So I sent for Bourne and asked him to join me. Deuced informal thing to do, but I'd not go alone with all that gold, and he's a good chap."

"Has Mr. Gifford been hurt?" she asked with a touch of concern.

Deveron flung himself in a chair and snorted. "You might say so, and his own doing. We all had a glass of brandy last night, farewell and all that, you know. We took ourselves upstairs except Gifford. Said he wanted to think. So surprised I left him. Woke up two hours later, saw lights, went down, and there he was in the armchair, brandy bottle nearly empty. I shook him, told him he'd be bosky in the morning."

" 'Drunk as a wheelbarrow now,' he told me, not displeased. Not like him, you know, so I asked why. He put up a hand and looked solemn as a parson. 'Four beautiful ladies,' he said, slow as a judge. Had to agree with him, of course, but asked what of it.

" 'Can't decide which one I love the most,' he went on, same solemn way, blurring his words. 'Know can't love four ladies at once but I do.' He drank what was in his glass. 'Can't decide which to take.'

" 'You ninnyhammer,' I shouted at him, 'won't any of them have you.'

" 'Oh, yes,' he nodded, 'they all will, all of 'em. I love 'em all. Got to decide which most. I'll tell you why.'

" 'No, you won't,' I said. 'You'll come to bed,' and tried to take his arm but he threw me off.

" 'I'll tell myself, then.' He smiled and picked up the brandy bottle. 'I'll finish this an' I'll tell. Go to bed, now, like a good lad, an' let me think.'

"I didn't want to brangle with him so I went off. This morning he was still in the chair, dead to the world. Took three of us to carry him up, so there's no riding for him." At that Deveron went into a whoop of laughter. "Wish you could have seen him, being so serious about the four ladies. No, as well you couldn't. But he's a splendid chap and a good friend. He'll have forgotten it all and I won't ride him. Know what? I think he's hung around Cordelia so long, never looked at other ladies, then had to look, and four at once overcame him. Can't blame him," and from his chair he made a bow. "Been overcome myself, but by three, not four." He stood up. "Well, I'll open that hole and be ready when Bourne gets here. Come along."

The library seemed stuffy and dim, and Thea went and threw open the bay windows to the sunlight and the terrace. Deveron brought the tools from the corner and together they pried up the stone until he could seize it and lift it to one side. The cavity lay empty. Deveron knelt, thrust in one hand, and brought out a scrap of leather. They sat back on their heels and looked at each other.

"What the devil?" He was half bewildered, half angry. "Where's our gold?"

Thea looked at him, at the empty hole, at the tools she had moved last night. That blow on her shoulder had not been of great vigor. "Wait," she gasped, and ran up to Ariel's room and was only half surprised to find it empty. Anger carried her back to the library, but there she began to laugh. "Oh, Myles, it is such a joke. We have been so bamboozled and utterly deceived. This morning—when she wasn't at breakfast I just thought she had left particularly early."

He took her shoulders and shook her. "Stop laughing. Tell me."

"We have been so neatly robbed. She was so innocent; we were so guileless we never suspected."

"I'll shake you again. What are you talking about? Where is the gold?"

"Gone—along with our little, demure, alleged cousin, Ariel," she gasped. "We were completely gulled by that little wench. You know it is a joke on us."

"I see no joke in losing eighty-five gold pieces. She stole them?"

"She did indeed. Her box is gone with her." She halted her laughter. "I don't think I could have stopped her."

"How stopped her? I swear I'll shake you."

"And I was almost beginning to think it was my own fault I stumbled." Half laughing, he lifted his hands and she told him quickly.

"You were brave to come down," he commended warmly. "Why?"

"The dust, and the tools." She pointed and gave another choke of laughter. "I thought they might be noticed if a servant came in early so I came to move them."

"I'm grateful it was she you interrupted and not her cousin. The little thief." He jumped up. "I'll set out after her. She can't take our gold."

"She probably thinks its hers—she said finders keepers." Thea began laughing again. "We were so kind. We gave her three pieces."

"They were staying at the inn. I'll go there first." He started to the door. Thea thought she heard a horse approaching and wondered who but the hoofbeats ceased. She scrambled up. "No, Myles. Come back. They'd have left in the dark of the night."

"She gave you her direction, I heard."

"And a false one, I'll wager. No, no. The gold is gone. We must be thankful she did not find the emeralds and admit that her finding the gold was remarkable. If you regard it properly it *is* a joke on us."

For a moment he looked as if he could not discover any joke, then reluctantly he grinned. "You're right. We welcomed her, called her cousin, which I'll wager she isn't, no matter how she looks. How could we . . . ?" He began to laugh. "We must never tell."

"But how sad we can't." Their faces alight with laughter they looked at each other with pleasure. "But," choked Thea, "I do not bear her ill will, do you? And we must admire how expertly she played her role."

"Granted, but I hate to have had the wool so pulled over our eyes. When I think on her manner . . ."

"And her voice, so shy and modest. She even told us she had a feeling the emeralds would some day be hers! She'd have stolen them, of course, but we would never have suspected that. How she must have been laughing inside at us all the time. It's our own secret."

"Yes." He looked her up and down, at the curling brown hair, the laughing hazel eyes. "Oh, Thea. You are a most endearing girl. My offer stands, you know. Any time. For I do truly love you." He leaned over and kissed her cheek.

"Dear Myles. I am happy it is with you with whom I share—so much. But let us wait and see. Remember," and her glance was roguish, "you have just finished saying there are three ladies you are in love with at once. How can I be sure your fancy will end with me?"

His eyes were as laughing as hers. "We may need to rescue each other. I do not know . . ."

"Of course you don't," she agreed cordially. "There is no need, yet. But, Myles . . ." something had come into her mind that she had thought of from time to time and in this moment of shared warm amusement she could ask, "why were you so odious to me at the beginning and for so long? You are, have been recently, so different."

He nodded, rose, picked up her hand, and led her to the small sofa. "I've wanted to explain," he said, "but no time ever seemed right until now. I knew I was behaving outrageously. But I could not stop myself. My consequence was quite new, you see, only for fourteen months had I had a title, an income, a place in society. Oh, I was not quite green, an officer in a good regiment learns quickly. I knew something of the polite world. But suddenly to be able to enter it in style! I see now I was green enough to wish to hide the fact I was green. I put on an air of hauteur such as I saw on some around me, became high in the instep, impressed my old friend Gifford. And then," he paused but his gaze did not waver, "I met and fell in love with Cordelia. She was so beautiful. . . . And those around her were of the ton, I felt I must make myself their equal, surpass them, to win her attention, her hand. She expects those manners, you know, and is repulsed by anything more informal. Once I tried to kiss her and she did not look at me for two weeks. All the while I was playing a part, but it nearly became part of me.

"And then, you were so drab looking, so young in appearance. I was affronted that I should be shackled with such a distressing creature. I wished to put you out of my sight as not a fitting companion or coheir. Then you showed you were not the meek child at all. Gifford pointed that out even then. When you returned from London you were quite different—which I could see but would not allow myself to realize. I understand myself more now than I did. But, oh, Thea, I am not sure of anything or of what I want. Which is shocking for a grown man to admit—but I don't. The army? No. Society? No. But travel now—I've listened to Ledgefield, Rushdon, Bourne, the Conde telling tales of far lands. I'd like to go see them."

"Dear Myles. You will. Now I understand I am in great charity with you. I was sadly set down, you must know, by your attitude. Now I am recovered." She smiled back at his anxious expression. "And if it took the gold to bring us to this understanding, I for one say it was worth it."

She paused, then frowned. "It is odd. When I swung that crowbar I felt it strike something. And I was being knocked over myself. But what did I hit? It must have made some damage, but it wasn't to Ariel. Nothing fell."

She got up and walked to the side of the chimney above the gaping hole. Sunlight lay on the plaster ornament, the gilded cornucopia spilling a bunch of red roses on the marble pilaster beside the fireplace. . . . Incongruously, Lucy held a red rose in her portrait. Thea went closer and peered. There was the gilt of the cornucopia, the scarlet and red of fat roses, and green of fat leaves. "Myles, come here," she cried. "See?" She pointed to a glint of green on the side of a rose. "That shouldn't be there."

"Why not? Lots of green."

"But not *in* a rose. Look." She stepped closer and

touched the spot. A piece of plaster, red on top, white underneath, fell into her hand. The green was larger. "Myles!"

His finger came beside hers and picked at the rose and more of the red fell away. They were looking at a glowing emerald, and, in a moment, at each other. "Hand me the chisel," he said hoarsely. "But I don't want to damage it."

Under his gentle, easy prying, the entire rose came away and two emeralds in an earring lay in his hand.

"Oooooh," sighed Thea. "We've found them."

"You have. They're yours. What shall we do with them?"

She put her hands to her cheeks. "If we take them now the decoration will be gone . . . it would be obvious what we have found. Let us try to fit back the stones and these pieces of red. I'll get a little water, a cloth." She turned to the door, found her knees shaking, and sat down on the floor abruptly. "No. It is too much. I'll go in a minute. But Myles, it's another joke. There the stones were, right above the gold, and Ariel never turned up her rod. Wouldn't she be *furious*?" She began to laugh, and his chuckle turned into a guffaw. "You're right. What a howler!"

"Don't you see? This frees us both." She turned to him eagerly. "We've found the things. We can do what we wish. We have Ardsley. And we don't have to get married to anyone."

He pulled his gaze from the emeralds to her face. "Don't have to get married? By Jove, you're right."

She laid a hand over his. "You don't really want to get married, do you?"

His smile was affectionate and amused. "Dear cousin, if I did I truly believe it would be you. But, no, I don't want to get married. Not to either of those two beauties. You are a dear and so right." He rose and stooping put his hands under her elbows and raised her to her feet. "Do you feel yourself? You have had a shock," he said seriously.

"Not such a shock that I am not now recovered," Thea reassured him. "I will get the water."

She was still laughing when she returned. By fitting the stones into their hole and the pieces of plaster over the space where moistened it seemed it would stay, they were sure no one would notice the new cracks in the plaster. Finishing, they sat down on the floor again to admire their handiwork and laugh again.

"But we must do something with them," began Deveron, hugging his knees. "We must inform Tillingbourne. But then what?"

Thea drew up her knees, it was really very comfortable, and swiveled around to face him. "Do you want them? They're half yours."

"Good Gad, no. What would I do with them? Though," he added a little wistfully, "they would look magnificent on Cordelia."

"Or on Costanza. You'd have to marry one of them."

"But how about you? Don't you truly want them?"

Thea shook her head. "What would I do with them? I am not of the stature, I do not have the presence to carry them with assurance. Once or twice a year would be the most I could wear them. And never at all in Dorset."

"Why Dorset, of all places?"

"When my time here is run, I will have to retire to some place where I can live on my yearly allowance. I have thought of Dorset with Cousin Susan."

It was Deveron's turn to laugh. "Then unthink Dorset, my girl. Your cousin will not be retiring there. Have you had no eyes these past days? Lord Ledgefield will make an offer any day now."

"Oh, dear. I have indeed been blind." For a moment

she looked disconcerted but. added, "Then I will have to think of something else."

"You can always marry, you know," he said seriously.

"The question remains—whom? I find that problematical." She paused and looked at the damaged rose nestling in its spray. "What about the emeralds? Since neither of us wishes to own them, what would you say if we gave them to Costanza? No one in the world would take more delight in possessing and wearing them."

His look was searching. "The thought crossed my mind, but it must be your wish. If it truly is, why, I am for it. Best thing in the world . . . restoring them to the family . . . yes. I'm for it. But we hold it a secret for the nonce."

She held out her hand. "Let us seal the bargain." They shook hands solemnly, and then both began to laugh helplessly.

"So you have everything settled and all but signed," remarked a quiet voice from the doorway. Bourne, in riding dress, was looking at them without expression. "You must forgive my entering unannounced. I heard such happy laughter as I was admitted that I told your footman I was expected and would join you."

Not at all thrown into confusion at being found seated on the floor, Thea held out her hand. Bourne stepped to her, reached for it and pulled her to her feet with what seemed to her unnecessary vigor. "Of course you do not need to be announced," she told him gaily. "You are always welcome." She glanced over her shoulder at Deveron who was rising. "We were laughing at many things." He dropped her hand and stepped back, his head on one side, regarding her steadily. "Among them," she went on in a rush, somehow disturbed by the bleak look in his eyes, "at the manner in which we have been gulled and robbed."

"What?" His eyebrows shot up and for the first time he looked at Deveron. "I came to ride with you . . . "

"Knew you would. Good of you, but no need now." Deveron began to laugh again.

Laughing herself and laying her hand on Bourne's arm, Thea led him to the corner of the hearth and pointed. "See."

He glanced into the hole. "The gold is packed and ready to be carried?" he asked politely.

"No, no." Deveron choked. "We came for it. That's what we found. Gold's gone."

"And your Ariel Kempton's gone, also, I wager." He could not resist joining their laughter. "I did wonder about her, but put the thought aside as incredible. But never had I thought to laugh at the loss of gold to a friend."

"We could not resist," gasped Thea. "Every time we thought how we had been gulled, all of us, we started again. She was so demure, so—so appreciative. I asked her to return to learn more of Ardsley and she accepted." She dabbed at her eyes. "I am laughing at myself the most. I thought I should do my duty by her."

"She was most plausible," agreed Bourne. "She did find the gold. And dowsing is a highly respected gift, you know."

Merrily she looked up at him, unconscious her hair was becomingly towsled and her curls falling. "Oh, Bourne, is it not a joke on us? But we must never let anyone know."

"No," he agreed, not taking his eyes from her face. "But perhaps there is a clue here." From his pocket he brought out a letter inscribed to Lord Deveron. "I met Tillingbourne's clerk on the road and undertook to delives this and save him part of his journey."

"Good of you." Deveron took it eagerly. "Come, let us sit at the table in more comfort." He broke the seal and spread the page. "I'll read it . . . My lord . . . and so on . . . 'I have distressing news to impart, and I must own to the deepest shame that I have been party to a gross deception, however unintended my share. When the young woman calling herself Anne Kempton came to my office and asked if she might go to see you and Miss Minturn, she bore a paper on which her parentage was given. Lord Stanford had known only the names of the mothers of the heirs. I saw no reason to doubt her and penned the note she carried to you. My deepest apologies.

" 'For now I have discovered she is an imposter. The true Anne Kempton is Mrs. William Hunnicutt. Her husband has a small holding not far from York. They have three children. By chance her pastor saw in an old London newspaper the account of Lord Stanford's death and the search for heirs. From Mrs. Hunnicutt's mother he had heard of the distant relationship and an account of a call at Ardsley Hall. I felt it incumbent upon me to journey to the village and am but now returned. I found the pastor an educated man. Mrs. Hunnicutt produced a family bible that held proof of the relationship. She and her husband are pleasant and superior to their present material situation.

" 'Furthermore, I discovered that the young person who came to us is in reality a Sophie Thwing who was for several years a neighbor. On learning of Mrs. Hunnicutt's connection, the Thwing girl plied her and her mother constantly with questions, and since the interest seemed harmless they told her what they knew. She left the district over three years ago, and I am told that, under her own name, she is known as an above-average successful dowser.

" 'I am convinced you would not care to punish this young person for imposture for the notoriety would be regrettable. But I strongly recommend that you and Miss Minturn send her instantly from Ardsley. With renewed apologies . . .' and he goes on to say how sorry he is. He better be! Isn't that a hum for him?" Deveron tossed the letter on the table.

"Of course it was the only chance for her to remove the gold," mused Thea. "I wish I'd been near enough to snatch some of that hair from her head. Not that I begrudge her the hair or the gold," she added hastily.

"What?" For the first time Bourne looked startled, so she had to tell her tale.

"Foolhardy to a fault, as usual," was his only comment. "You are fortunate you came out of it so well, since you say your shoulder was only bruised. Are you going to pursue the girl, Deveron?"

"How can I?" Deveron spread his hands and gave the reasons it was not possible. "Besides," he added with an air of magnanimity, "Thea and I cannot bring ourselves to seek her or the gold. We are agreed on this."

"And on many other things," commented Bourne colorlessly. "You are right. You could never find her."

"She'll dye her hair," Thea gurgled, "or perhaps it was dyed already, and put on rouge . . . but I must stop reflecting . . ."

"No one who was here will be so unmannerly as to ask what we have done with those ducats so it can all be put away and covered with clean linen," Deveron said seriously. "At least you and I, Bourne, are spared a ride to London today."

"You will be removing soon?"

"Oh, indeed, in time for Lady Jersey's ball. We will have a surprise for that occasion," Thea said merrily.

"Then I will count on seeing you there." Bourne rose. "My felicitations, both of you, on your good sense." Bowing, he left.

"Now what did he mean by that?" wondered Thea.

"Oh, that we're not raising the wind over the treasure. He has odd humors at times, I've noticed." He rose in turn. "Must get back and see how Gifford is doing."

"Since you are here you can escort Cordelia up tomorrow, or even drive her yourself." Thea gave him a sideways glance.

"Viper," he grinned. "I'll not leave the place until the next day. We must decide how best to approach Costanza."

". . . and make her happy beyond words." Thea regarded him seriously. The eyelids no longer drooped over the blue eyes, the dark hair was no longer in the windswept style, he was smiling and his whole face so animated it was entirely different from the one she had first seen.

"Yes. There must be some kind of display about it. Costanza has hidden her purpose in coming to England but not refrained on occasion to repeat the tale of her ancestress, with embellishments of a most lurid nature about Sir Richard. Once seen, it will be obvious what the necklace is." The dark brows drew together in thought.

"But the perfect opportunity is before us," Thea cried. "The ball of Lady Jersey! We, you and I together, will take the necklace to Costanza just before she leaves for the ball. And with you to escort her, there can be no doubt in the mind of any beholder that the Zamora emeralds have been discovered and returned to their rightful owner."

His look was admiring. "Splendid. All will be overcome! But . . . but . . . if I escort her and she has the emeralds from Ardsley, will it appear that I have offered for her? I should not care for that."

"Oh, no, I should not think so. Fernando will escort me. It will appear a family affair . . . and that justice has been done. It will be the talk of the evening, and Lady Jersey will be delighted to have such a coup."

"It will be another on dit we'll have furnished, cousin. I'll have to tell Gifford, but he's mum as a flounder. Two days from now we'll come and take them out of that plaster, and I'll carry them to town and have them cleaned quickly. I'll tell Tillingbourne on the way. I'll come for you, with them, two hours before the opening of the ball.

Do you arrange for Costanza to await us?"

"Gladly. We will leave here just after you. I will have to tell Brewton, for the ornament there will be in pieces, but he will be able to think of something to tell the servants to account for the damage far better than I could. That decoration probably cannot be repaired, but that is a problem I will confront later."

"Yes, forget that for now. May Gifford and I call this evening? It will be pleasant just to entertain ourselves. I almost wished to inform Bourne just now, but decided to astound him with the others. He is a most accomplished man by the way, which one would not always suspect, and has been of help to me during this entertaining. Here, I better return these tools, no, I'll give them to Brewton to have that done." He picked them up from the floor. "Cousin, I thank you for the most remarkable morning of my life." He gave her a salute with the chisel, laughed, and left.

Fourteen

AN HOUR before the opening of Lady Jersey's ball, the Ardsley coach drew up at the entrance of the mansion on Berkeley Square. Lord Deveron assisted Thea to alight, then handed a flat box to the footman who bore it up the steps behind them. At the door Deveron took it from him and followed Thea and the butler up to the saloon where they waited.

"Found just the right box to hold the things," he whispered to her. "They look even better cleaned. Sure you aren't regretting the gift?"

Her gaze was solemn. "Yes, I am, a little. And green is a shade I can wear, though I truly prefer blue, except that is taken by all blondes. But I know the emeralds are not right for me, so I am only a little sorry."

"You're a top-notch girl, Thea. Don't know another who'd be so calm about giving away a fortune, or who would even think of bestowing one on someone else. Since blue is your preference, I'll bring you some sapphires from India some day. They'd become you."

"What a kind but impossible thought," she glowed at him. "But . . ."

Costanza rushed into the room. "Dear friends. How amiable of you to come to escort us. Though why Thea specified I should wear white is beyond imagining. But it is delightful to see you."

She looked more magnificent than usual in a white satin embroidered in gold and wore a gold chain of sprays set with tiny diamonds. Fernando, also in white with a canary waistcoat, followed, murmuring his welcome. Thea wished again she could have worn a blue gown but told herself she was wise not to compete with the blondes since they had an unvarying partiality for blue, and knew her Nile green with tiny leaves embroidered in gold suited her almost as well.

"Thea." Deveron spoke rather sharply. "Stop thinking of something else. We must do this together." She jumped and looked at him fondly and thought he, too, looked more handsome than ever.

"Of course." She went to stand by his side.

"I, as you must guess, Costanza, am not one to make speeches," he began a little awkwardly. "But we, Thea and I, have a gift for you. It is something we have found, and we are bestowing it on you as from our family to yours, to right an ancient wrong." He ended in a rush and carried across the flat green velvet box and put it in her hands.

"Oh, no!" Eyes and mouth opened wide. She looked down, pressed the catch, and the Zamora emeralds glowed on the white velvet of the lining.

"No!" cried Fernando, and sprang to take the box from her shaking hands. "It is not possible."

Costanza lifted out the necklace. From a single strand at either side, square stones spread in a wide elaborate gold setting of several strands that joined in a curve carrying a yet larger drop from the center. As it hung a moment, each stone glowed in the light in a constellation of sparkling green fire. "How beautiful!" she breathed, and looked at the two. "You are giving it to me!"

"Restoring it," Deveron said complacently and beamed at Thea. Almost bemused, Costanza raised her arms to unfasten the gold necklace and drop it on the floor while Fernando held the emeralds, then taking that, she fastened it in place. The stones shone against her white skin, and she seemed to grow taller. I was right, Thea thought a little sadly, they would not do for me, but it would have been a pleasure to look at them. The bracelets were four stones wide, like cuffs, the earrings, fastened in place of the gold ones, were a chain of two that dropped from a large button.

"Oh, on you they are magnificent," Thea gasped in wholehearted admiration.

"Yes." Costanza moved to regard herself in one of the long mirrors. "Yes. And they are beautiful beyond belief. Oh, my dear friends, I have no words to tell you of my gratitude." She paused and nodded to the mirror solemnly. "Never did I think to see them, in truth." She whirled away, threw her arms around Thea and then around Deveron and whirled back to the mirror, laughing with excitement. Fernando kissed Thea on both cheeks and took both of Deveron's hands in both of his. "No words," he murmured.

"And you brought them for me to wear tonight!" Costanza cried. "You thought of everything. If only my grandmother knew!"

"Father will be very happy," Fernando pointed out prosaically, but his eyes were full of love and admiration as he watched his sister.

"But you, Thea." Costanza whirled back again. "You have no necklace!"

"Never had one nor felt the lack," Thea said cheerfully.

"But that is not right. Fernando, pick up the gold one, the earrings. These I give you, Thea—no, not as a

return but to remind you of me and my everlasting gratitude." Over protests she adjusted necklace and earrings
as Thea smiled, a little mistily, with pleasure.

"Right, Costanza," Deveron approved, "just the thing
for her."

"And now," Costanza tossed her head, put up one
hand to feel the earrings, admired the bracelet as she
lowered it, "we must go to this dear Lady Jersey so we
will arrive neither too early nor too late."

Lady Jersey was still receiving, though the hour was
a little advanced, when the four were announced. Her
welcoming smile turned into a little shriek, louder than
customary, at the sight of Costanza, head high but with
the properly unconscious air, on the arm of Deveron.
"The emeralds!" the Lady gasped and shrieked again so
all heads turned. Costanza made a most stately curtsey
and Deveron his best bow.

"But how, when?" demanded Lady Jersey avidly. "What
a surprise. You wicked things. You should have told me.
I am quite unmanned."

"Never that, my lady," murmured Deveron and she
laughed loudly and tapped him with her fan.

Costanza bent her head a little. With her curls piled on
top of her head there was nothing to distract the gaze from
her and her necklace. "Miss Minturn, Lord Deveron," she
said a little aloofly, "have found the famous emeralds that
their family stole from mine and have bestowed them on
me now, as a rightful return."

Thea thought she might have put it a little more tactfully, but it was Costanza's triumph, and of course in
essence she was right. And she found herself hoping
Bourne was present and had seen the entrance.

"Go and dance, my loves." Lady Jersey was waving
them away. "I will send for you for I must hear everything.
You have quite made my party, for no one will stop talk-

ing, and that always signifies they are enjoying themselves even if what they say is the utmost nonsense. If one of the Royals does not appear you will take supper with me. Now I will look wise, as if I had known all along." She gave her laugh again and turned to those waiting in line.

Fernando was an excellent waltzer and did not expect conversation, so Thea felt free to gaze about the room whenever she could conceal that activity. Costanza and Deveron were waltzing sedately and were quite the handsomest couple in the room. Cordelia, eyes lowered, was with the fresh-faced Lord Herlwin. Around the walls, dowagers were whispering behind their fans. In one alcove Lady Erica and Mrs. Farraby were talking with great animation while Bourne leaned against the wall beside them and watched the scene. So he had been here . . . She gave Fernando a bright smile and became conscious he had been thanking her again for what they had done for his sister. "It means more than you can imagine," he was ending gravely. "Now she will be free to love, to marry, to have a happy life. I am forever in your debt, for I realize, as she may not, that the emeralds would have been yours, and it is you who have so generously parted with them."

She also turned serious. "But I was glad to. Deveron and I decided it was only right. And we are fond of your sister."

"No others would have been so generous," he told her as he led her to Mrs. Farraby. Bourne had disappeared.

"You've taken the wind out of every galleon and fishing smack in the room," Lady Erica said energetically. "You are quite mad and quite wrong to give up those emeralds, you know. But I suppose Susan has so informed you."

"Not at all," Mrs. Farraby contradicted placidly. "My opinion was not sought, but if it had been I would have agreed with Thea. Don't humph at me, Erica, for you know it was proper as well as generous."

Hurrying over, Deveron snatched her hand. "Ladies, your servant. Come on, Thea. It's a country dance and I will be able to work off some of my spirits. Knocked their teeth down their throats," he added happily as they went to the set. "Now, don't forget the story about how you found them."

"I know Lady Jersey will demand it, but it makes me a little unhappy that a portion is pure fabrication," she said a little apprehensively.

"Nonsense." He was robustly encouraging. "You tell a good story. And only a small portion is not true and think of the coil we'd be in if you did tell the truth. Laugh, now, this is a lively figure."

Captain Rushdon, her next partner, did not press for an account and soberly praised the action of the cousins. Mr. Gifford's exuberance was as overwhelming as his energy in the dance.

"Bang up to the nines, both of you," he told her as they met and parted. "Trust you to do the right thing." During a promenade he did say more soberly it was a pity the whole story couldn't be told but understood why not. "Almost sorry for Cordelia," he confided a few minutes later. "That necklace would look well on her too. But I wouldn't give a groat for her chances of trapping him now."

"Lord Herlwin seems deeply enamored," Thea said.

"Oh, he is. Good family and competence. She'll take him. But he aint Deveron and his place aint Ardsley. She's been picky too long. Not sure I'll dance with her."

"Oh, but you must. It would be cruel if you did not, after all these years."

"Why, yes, I suppose." He was surprised at the idea. "Glad you pointed that out. Kind. Always did like you. Once Deveron said I should make a push for you myself so the four of us could live at Ardsley."

"How kind of him." Her tone was icy.

"Yes. Wasn't it?" No sarcasm could reach Mr. Gifford. "I told him you were a taking little thing, particularly when in the high boughs. He didn't see it then. Does now, though."

"How kind," Thea gasped again. "What happened?" and had to wait for an answer.

"You need more than me in a husband. You're clever. I'm not. Didn't know how to go about fixing my interest. Felt ten years younger when Deveron said I didn't need to. Like you, you know. But we wouldn't suit."

"I fear you are right," she agreed seriously. "And there is your long devotion to Cordelia."

"Waste of time," he said simply. "Hopeless. Just followed the fashion. But," struck by a thought, "perhaps not. Kept me from being caught by anyone else. But I'll dance with her." On that promise he took her to Mrs. Farraby.

She found Bourne in front of her, a sardonic look in his eyes and a grim set to his firm mouth. As the music started he put his arm around her for a waltz and, when she started to protest that it was promised, merely tightened his arm. "Don't be freakish. I am taking this dance." He moved her away from an approaching figure. "That was quite an entrance you four made. Not a feather in a head-dress moved. Lady Cowley stopped in mid-sentence. Couldn't have arranged it better myself. How'd you find them?"

He swung her expertly, and she realized again there was more pleasure to be had dancing with him than with any other man. "Not going to tell me, eh? I want the real story, not what you've fixed up between you."

"I can't here, now," she said with a lilt of laughter. "Sometime, perhaps. It was really—nothing."

"Coming too strong, ma'am. Don't believe a word. Have it your way for now, but I'll see I get it later." He fell silent and his tone of raillery departed. "So you've accomplished what you set out to do from the beginning."

"What do you mean?" She tried to lean away from him, but his arm held her implacably.

"Don't try to play innocent with me. You always planned to get Deveron away from Cordelia."

Frowning a little, she looked up into the lean face attractive even in its grimness. "No, I don't think so," she began slowly. "Not right at the beginning. Though I did know quite quickly that she was not the proper wife for him or for Ardsley."

"He wouldn't have known that if you hadn't shown him."

"But I didn't. You make me sound so calculating. I didn't plan. If your Costanza hadn't come, he'd not have learned."

"Not my Costanza. She was just chance, but a help to you in that respect anyway. So now you have Ardsley. Are you happy?"

"I don't know." Suddenly she was wide-eyed and thoughtful.

"Can't you make up your mind?" His tone was jeering. "I know you have, so don't try to bamboozle me." He paused, then added carefully, "I must compliment you, Miss Minturn, on having turned out to be not only a most stylish young lady fitted to any position, but a much more interesting person than you first appeared. You saw to it that you gave me quite a different picture from the worldly being you are."

She would have liked to tread on his foot in exasperation but knew he would retaliate in kind. "What *are* you talking about?" she demanded hotly.

"Gently, now," he soothed in his most exasperatingly lofty manner. "One does not show any emotion in public. You appeared—and I confess I was quite taken in—to be gentle, unassuming, kind, unaffected, and intelligent."

"And you are telling me I am not all that now? Why you are insufferable, abominable. . . ."

"Quite. But change your expression for Lady Jersey has sent Deveron to take you to her table. My most humble thanks for an exceedingly interesting dance." She had turned her back as his bow was finished.

It took a strong effort of will to pull her mind back from that conversation and prepare for the interrogation that awaited her, and she was relieved to have a few minutes at the table while her hostess laughed and rallied with those who passed her. But when the food was brought, Lady Jersey fixed her with her large and handsome eyes. "Now, tell me how you found the famous emeralds," she commanded. "I must know, you understand, for already I am being quizzed as though I have long been privy to it all."

"I do not know myself, ma'am," cried Costanza across the table. "Only this evening did they appear."

"Indeed? And now, Miss Minturn . . ."

Thea and Deveron had devised a tale that held as much of the truth as possible. She had gone to the library and noticing, she thought, some dust on one of the silver candelabra on the mantel, she had lifted it down to determine if the footman should be reprimanded. The candelabra had proved heavier than she had realized. She could not hold it in one hand, it had overbalanced and had crashed into the plaster decoration of roses on a panel beside the fireplace, and then fallen to the hearth along with some pieces of red plaster. Aghast at the damage, she looked at the demolished cornucopia and roses, went closer, and saw the gleam of green within the remnants of the plaster where no green should be. She had sent for Deveron and together they had removed as much of the decoration as necessary to free the entire set of emeralds. Obviously it was where Sir Richard himself had hidden the emeralds for it had been remarked that he had enjoyed watching the

Italian workmen he had brought in to decorate some of the rooms of the Hall. After consulting, most seriously, they had decided it belonged by right to Costanza."

"Bravo!" cried Lady Jersey at the end and clapped her hands.

"Most admirable!" Across the table an older gentleman waved his glass, fortunately half empty, at them. "Upholding the honor of England," and drained his glass. Thea was gratified at this approval on such a high level of their deed and its patriotism and wished Bourne could have heard.

Lady Jersey gave a nod of approval. "An excellently told account. Miss Minturn, Deveron, I congratulate you both on all your actions. There, now, finish your plates, and make way for Lady Sefton and Mr. Alvanley. I must tell them." She smiled graciously and the four arose and departed.

But Thea found the remainder of the evening lacking in savor. The surprise, the *coup de foudre*, was over. Captain Rushdon, expressing a nearly fervent hope that she would remember him when he came back from the war, informed her he must return to his regiment in a few days. Bourne did not approach her again. And when they were at the house Cousin Susan came to her boudoir with undisguised happiness to announce that, since Thea was now provided with Ardsley, she would accept the flattering offer from Lord Ledgefield and looked forward to managing him and his estate in Herefordshire. Thea was able to say all the right things, but in the end she cried herself to sleep.

"Ralph and I will await your convenience, dear Thea," Cousin Susan said over breakfast. There was an open air of contentment about her. "Now that you and Deveron are not compelled to marry, as I understood the lawyer's words that afternoon, there can be no rush on that score.

But you will need some one to live with you, of course, and I will be most concerned to help you find an agreeable person. Or," she paused delicately, "have you anything else in mind?"

"No." Thea picked up her fork and put it down. She was feeling languid and not herself, doubtless from the late night and the excitement. "I cannot speak for Deveron except that he has indicated he is not intending to offer for Cordelia. I have no plans."

"I am happy for Deveron. But you, Captain Rushdon has been attentive beyond the normal of good manners," Cousin Susan offered.

"He tells me he is called to rejoin the army."

Cousin Susan made a little sound as of distress. "Then . . ."

"Lord Deveron and Mr. Tillingbourne beg that you will forgive the early hour of their call and do them the favor of meeting with them in the saloon, ma'am," announced the butler.

Since it was nearly noon it did not seem too early to Thea, but she hurried across the hall. The red saloon was somber, for no morning sun entered, and she almost sent for candles, but both men looked so serious she believed they would not wish to wait. They bowed. Deveron came to take her hand and lead her to the sofa, and, sitting down beside her, gestured to the lawyer to take a chair.

"Mr. Tillingbourne has brought us some information," his lordship began. "He tells me you will wish to be seated while you hear it."

Nothing that could be that serious came to Thea's mind, so she smiled at each one and said it was a pleasure to see them.

Mr. Tillingbourne cleared his throat and put a folder of papers on the table beside him. "This is almost as distressing for me as for you, for I fear the blame devolves on me for not making more clear an aspect of the late Lord Stanford's will."

"I, we," she glanced at Deveron, "have not thought of it again since that afternoon. But it seemed clear at the time."

"But not adequately, ma'am." He coughed and shifted the papers, then peered at them. "I did not inform his lordship of the cause of my arrival since I felt it better to see you together. In short, yesterday morning, on my return from a night in the country with a client, a note was waiting me from his lordship telling he and you had found the Zamora emeralds, one of the conditions, he pointed out, of the will, and that the finding of the emeralds meant that Ardsley Hall would remain in your divided possession without other condtions. I am most curious as to how and where you found them, but that can wait. I had intended to ride to the Hall that day to express my chagrin in person over the imposture of that young female which I so unwittingly abetted, but no matter. His lordship's note also informed me that he was carrying the emeralds to London and that you and he would present them to the Condesa de Villamayo, the descendant of the original owner, the next evening.

"As to that I have now inquired. Lord Deveron has told me that you, Miss Minturn, and he, did indeed bestow the emeralds on the Condesa and that she wore the complete set, to the astonishment of all, at a ball given by Lady Jersey. I had hoped to reach London before dinner to warn you, but I was delayed, a horse lamed, not another available, it was nearly midnight when I reached my hotel. By then the deed was done."

"Yes. We took the set to her before the ball, as I told you. It seemed to us only proper and in justice to return them." Deveron's eyes were narrowed.

"Justice and propriety had not entered the mind of Lord Stanford when he made his will. He did not believe,

I must allow, that the emeralds would ever be found. But there was a chance, and he was a gambler who would not overlook odds. He put in the will that if you found the emeralds and thereby increased the wealth and consequence of the family, Ardsley Hall would indeed be yours. You found them. But by bestowing them on the Condesa you have removed them from the family possession and have not, therefore, increased the wealth and consequence of the family of Lord Stanford to any degree."

Mr. Tillingbourne dropped a little of his official manner. "So it appeared to me as I reread the portion of the will. But I would not trust my own judgment. This morning I carried the will and consulted with Lord Debinghurst, perhaps the most eminent lawyer of the kingdom on the matter of wills, with whom I have slight acquaintance, and laid the will and the problem before him. It is his opinion, and it is not likely anyone could be found to dispute it, that though you have complied with one provision you have failed on the other, and the most important. It is his further opinion that you have forfeited the right to Ardsley Hall and that this would be true even if you should both marry in accordance with another provision. He pointed out that if you were already married the problem might well be moot, and a decision might be in doubt. But since you have not complied with any provisions of the late Lord Stanford's will, there can be no doubt that by giving away such an asset of the estate, and in defiance of the provision, Ardsley is no longer yours, and you will be required to leave when your original period of six months has expired."

His expression changed to one almost of anguish and he wrung his hands. "Oh, my dear young people. Forgive me. I have come to like and respect you both. My distress at being compelled so to inform you is beyond measure. But a lawyer is bound by the wishes of his client. I have no recourse."

"Yes, of course," Thea faltered, but the enormity of what was happening enlarged before her. "Oh, Myles," she turned and put both hands on his arm. Anger and bewilderment struggled on his face. "I fear this is my fault. I suggested we bestow them on Costanza."

"I'd thought of it, said so." His other hand came over hers. "I agreed. I didn't have to. Never thought of anything else, really. I should have. Thea, I was a fool."

"No, no," Mr. Tillinghouse was moaning. "Nobility of character . . . generous to a fault. . . ."

"Just being honest," Deveron exploded. "It seems damned smokey to me." He jumped up, fists clenched, and paced to the window. "Here we find the things no one else has been able to and give them where they belong and get kicked out for our trouble."

"I should have warned you." Mr. Tillingbourne wrung his hands again. "It never crossed my mind the emeralds would appear. It is most unjust." He moaned.

"It's not only unfair, it's damned awkward, too." Deveron's voice started to rise but he stopped it and paced again, his face flushed and his hands clenched. But quickly he mastered his emotions and returned to sit beside Thea. "Here our friends, everyone, all congratulating us on having secured the Hall, expecting us to settle down, take our places in the county, in town." His voice was a little hoarse but even. "And next month they'll find some yokels in our places."

"No. Not yokels, superior people, they will learn," protested Mr. Tillingbourne feebly. "But the force of your observations is overwhelming."

Deveron turned grim. "It nigh overwhelms me. What to say, do?"

"You will doubtless wish to return to Ardsley immediately." Mr. Tillingbourne stopped wringing his hands. "All must be informed."

"No!" Thea had been half listening, half thinking, and

this last assumption put up her hackles. She stamped her foot and both looked at her in amazement. "We are not so poor-spirited as you assume, sir."

"But there is so little time. . . ."

"Time for what? Do you mean to turn us out before our alloted span? No. That I will not allow. Deveron and I are not ones to run away."

"No, by Jove." Deveron's face lightened. "We have two . . . three weeks, after all. Go on, Thea."

She looked at him, at the lawyer. "No one knows of this but you and your prohibiting friend, sir? Then there is no reason why it should be revealed until the last moment when it is necessary, and," she added thoughtfully, "perhaps not then. You have no control over our actions."

"Certainly not, ma'am, certainly not. But . . . the will . . ."

"Keep quiet while I think. You and your will. . . ." She turned sideways to Deveron. "There is no need to reveal this provision or anything else at this time. What I propose is that we remain in town to enjoy our fame and the pleasures of society for at least two more weeks. Towards the end of that time we can begin to put it about that we neither of us are so enamored of Ardsley that we wish to be coerced into marriage, since neither of us has found the partner we truly desire. We do not countenance the yielding up of . . . of our freedom, of our choice of action. We will then, both of us, depart from the Hall in dignified and seemly fashion and will be so removed from gossip and backbiting and malice that nothing can touch us, and the furor, if any, will soon die down. What do you say, Myles?"

He patted her hand and laughed. "I might have known you would find a way for us to come about. There could be nothing better. And it follows an idea of my own I'll tell you later. But Cordelia . . ." His brow wrinkled. "I'll have to tell her. Couldn't fail in that, after all this time, you know. But she'll keep mum."

"Oh, she will," Thea assured him. "It would be lowering for her if it was revealed. And when she finds half of Ardsley is no longer yours, she will feel it is your just desserts for the attentions you paid Costanza, but she will weep a little, prettily, and happily accept Lord Herlwin."

"You're right," and his smile broadened. "And she'll not be on my conscience for I've had a devilish time figuring how to get out of that thicket, I can tell you. So," he stopped smiling and turned in a lordly manner to face Mr. Tillingbourne. "We thank you, sir, for your efforts to warn us in time and for your consideration in obtaining a further opinion and your distress at the announcement you were forced to make. You will tell no one now nor, do I advise, in the future, of that provision in the will. The fact that neither of us has married will be reason enough for the world to know as the cause of our departure from Ardsley. Do you agree?"

Mr. Tillingbourne, back in his place as the lawyer to a noble lord, bowed, "As you wish, my lord, I will tell no one, now or ever. And I thank you and Miss Minturn for receiving the news in a manner that shows you do not hold me in any blame. I assure you I will see that I, and my successors, will attend with great care to the affairs of the Stanford estate." He bowed and rose. "With your permission, I will leave." He bowed again and walked out, a little stiffly.

"Poor chap," Deveron became tolerant, "he really was distressed about all that. But he'll manage the new heirs and enjoy himself more than he would have with us."

"Yes, but he'll miss the consequence you brought," Thea gurgled suddenly. "And how he would have been beaten to the ground if we had told him of the gold."

"He'd probably have found a clause to blame us for that, too. All you propose now is sensible, and I agree and thank you. We've had a good run for our money, haven't we? And we each will be sent that yearly allowance from the trust. I'll stop next week to see him, no, the last week, and make sure there's no doubt about that. But . . ." He rose and began to pace, paused and looked at her seriously. "How about you? You've no place to go. You won't take Rushdon, eh? I hear he's rejoining his regiment. Your Cousin . . . but if she hasn't already taken Ledgefield, she will. You won't have a place to lay your head."

That aspect had not occurred to Thea, and she gasped. "Why, you're right. I won't even have a spot to build a wattle-hut, isn't that what the homeless do? I will have to tell Cousin Susan in any event. I'll go down to her cottage in Dorsett and decide there what I must do next."

"Too bad to bury yourself." He stood before her and looked down. "You're devilish attractive now, you know, even if not in the accepted mode. You need to meet more men, find one who'd appreciate you." He held out his hand.

"Dear Myles." She put her hand in his, and he pulled her up from the sofa. "You are coming over sweet to make me feel better. But I've had a season and have not taken to such a degree that I have any confidence in myself."

"Stupid," he said roundly. "It wasn't a fair test. All sorts of things against you. There were enough fortune hunters hovering, I turned some away, too. Trouble was you never put your mind to it, as the other girls do, too interested in too much. But you always have found the way out of a coil. You'll come about. In the meantime, let us enjoy these last days of our consequence."

Fifteen

IT WAS no surprise that the two weeks passed quickly for Thea. She and Deveron were deluged with attentions from friends and acquaintances and lived in a whirl of gaiety from noon to midnight. But though the popularity and compliments could but be enjoyed, there was the frequently near-impertinent curiosity to be evaded, and she found she could not feel the wholehearted pleasure she had anticipated. She reminded herself she would never again be in London on such terms and set herself resolutely to find every crowded day and evening supremely delightful.

At the first Assembly at Almack's following the ball of Lady Jersey, Thea was amused that Deveron danced twice with Cordelia and with Costanza. He favored Thea for a lively country dance during which he revealed that he was enjoying himself as never before, and perhaps it was fortunate it would not last for no one could keep to his pace for long.

Bourne appeared, watched without evident interest, danced once with each of the two beauties, and then took Thea into a waltz. He complimented her on her appearance—she had bravely worn her favorite blue with an embroidered gauze overskirt and the necklace from Costanza —and expressed most formally the hope she was enjoying her triumphs of so many kinds, then turned aloof, refusing to respond to her attempts to engage his interest. Receiving the same tight smile after her third effort, and losing patience, she raised the hand on his shoulder high enough to enable her to bring it down on edge and had the satisfaction of feeling him start.

"Stop giving me that steely smile." She was out-of-reason angry. "You once raked me over the coals for not appearing to enjoy my partner's words. You are looking like a—a lamp post and behaving with a shocking want of gallantry."

"You always do find the unusual comparison, Miss Minturn," he returned urbanely, but he did look down at her. "I am quite sunk below reproach."

"Flummery. Though your conduct does veer like a sailboat without a rudder. If you had no intention of enjoying this dance, you should not have asked me."

"I always do my duty," he murmured, and his head came down a little, "even when it presents . . . problems. You better laugh now instead of flying into a pet, gives a better appearance."

A little spurt of laughter escaped her. "Oh, Bourne, I can never stay angry with you." For a moment his arm tightened. "And even if your duty was abhorrent to you, I am glad you asked me, for you are quite the best waltzer in the room."

"You are a minx," and his voice was a shade warmer. "I must rise to that lure and return the compliment." His arm loosened. "Stop trying to put me to the blush. And I warn you, never again do you hit a partner on the dance floor."

"I knew you wouldn't mind, and I had to bring you out of the sullens, and I did." She gave him a merry glance. "You are enjoying the dance more now, you must admit."

"Sparring with you is always delightfully entertaining. I regret future opportunities will be so few."

"Why?" she demanded. He must be reminding her of the end of her stay at Ardsley, which was hardly kind.

He only gave her an enigmatic look as he dropped his arm and then removed her hand from his shoulder. "The music has stopped, in case you have not noticed. My gratitude for the dance." He bowed and led her firmly, without another word, to her cousin.

He did not appear at Lady Mofton's rout two nights later, and Deveron let drop he had gone on a visit to Gloucestershire. Unless he returned soon, she would not see him again. Indeed, she might never see him again. She found that dismaying and had to take herself in hand; she must not allow herself to be so cast down and must banish him from her thoughts.

The Villamayos departed from London the next week. The leave-taking was highly emotional on the part of Costanza, who kept bursting into tears, while Fernando repeatedly pressed for a promise of a visit as soon as possible—until Thea was quite distracted and relieved to see Deveron escort them to their coach. Cousin Susan was most unhappy about Thea's loss of a home and, after offering her one in Herefordshire at any time, told her to use the cottage near Swanage for as long as she desired. There was a friend, a most agreeable maiden lady who would surely come and stay with Thea. It sounded dreary, but Thea accepted with all the gratitude she could muster. Then, on the last day in London, she found she was happy it was all over—the false interest, the prying endeavors to learn her plans, her own delicate evasions—and at that last ball she felt, and knew she showed, high spirits.

Deveron and she had agreed they must inform the Brewtons of their change of circumstance and enlist their aid and silence until the last day. The first morning at Ardsley she summoned them to the library and told them the reasons for the departure, enjoining secrecy and asking them to give about the version they themselves had made public these past two weeks. The unhappiness and sense of outrage the Brewtons freely expressed moved her almost to tears. She put off packing, for though she could not imagine what she could do with her gowns in Dorset, she could not leave them behind; she took her favorite walks and was grateful to her cousin for her silence about their futures and her matter-of-fact acceptance of the present. Mr. Tillingbourne had at last discovered a struggling young lawyer in Liverpool, married, with a child, who was the cousin to follow Deveron, and was well satisfied with him and his possibilities. Also he had found an Italian decorator and persuaded him to come and replace the damaged flowers by the fireplace in the library. It was more skillfully executed than the mate, but Thea was sure no one would notice or in any way suspect the part the plaster ornament had played in family history. She was not sorry to leave Ardsley, she told herself frequently, but surely a certain amount of regret could be considered proper and permissible.

Deveron arrived after dinner the next evening, looking very pleased with himself. "Everything shipshape Bristol fashion," he announced, taking a chair. "Told my people. My man's packing. Have two prime things to tell you."

He got up and walked around as though his spirits were so high he could not stay still for long. "You were right again, Thea. I shall miss you, you know. But to tell you . . . I made a call on Cordelia yesterday afternoon. She was miffed I was not taking her driving but that soon passed. Put it to her just as you advised, enough of the truth to render her comfortable as to my attentions in the past—but—no more Ardsley as neither of us wishes to marry. I must admit I put a little emphasis on you . . .

never saw her cry before but she did, a very little. Regretted that infamous will, had enjoyed my company, would never forget me, and then, do you know, she was stupid enough to say that she was particularly disappointed at not having the redecoration of my half of Ardsley, for she had so enjoyed the planning! That knocked down my pretensions, and I told her so, which embarrassed her to such a high degree she had not fully recovered when I left. A lesson to her, I hope. I'm well out of that."

"How splendidly you managed," Thea gurgled.

"I would have been free in time," he said largely, "just needed to have my eyes opened, you know. But the other surprise . . ." He got up again and came and sat beside her on the sofa. "It distresses me deeply, please believe, Thea, to go off and leave you at this juncture. What will you do?"

"Cousin Susan is lending me her cottage. I will do famously," she told him firmly. "What are you doing?"

"Going to India." His tone was triumphant. "Told you once that Ledgefield talked about it, Rushdon, too; they're both giving me letters. Fabulous place, India—tigers, maharajahs, palaces. Gifford's coming with me. It will be splendid. When I've seen all I want, I'll go on somewhere new. I'll write you, care of Tillingbourne. I stopped by him today, and he promises all is in train for our allowances. But think, Thea, I've got the whole world to see. I know you would like to come, too, just what would appeal to you. Tell you what, when I come back, oh, in a year or two, I'll come see you, have to bring those sapphires anyway, discover how things are between us, eh? You're a delightful girl, and I know I was lucky you were the other heir." He kissed her cheek and rose. "Must look to the packing. Gifford sent his regards and farewells, by the way. Going up tomorrow." He paused and some of his exuberance left him as he looked at her anxiously. "Are you sure you're going to be all right? Yes? Well, then, I wish you so very well, and—and good-bye, dear cousin." To her surprise he stooped and kissed her again and hurried from the room.

Thea found she was crying, because he was going out of her life, because she would be truly alone, and because there was no one to whom she could turn even to ask the time of day, and she cried her way upstairs and to sleep.

One of Thea's delights at Ardsley had been riding Dawn. Until she began packing the only thing she could do at the Hall now was to wander around and try not to regret she was leaving. So the next morning a ride was indicated. She mounted at the stables and walked the filly around to the front. She would take another look at the imposing gatehouse, the incongruous wings, the first view she had had of the place. She reined to a halt in spite of Dawn's objections and as she did heard a horse trotting nearby. One of the grooms exercising one of the horses, she thought, and gazed up at the ramparts on top of the towers.

"Good morning, Miss Minturn," said a voice just behind her. "Taking an admiring look at your home?"

"What?" She turned, astonished, for she had not thought to see Lord Bourne again.

"When you were not at the river this morning I came for you. You and I are going to have a talk." He was maneuvering his big black so close to Dawn that the filly started to fidget. Then he was touching on the left, one arm reached out and around her waist, the other caught her under the knees, and she was lifted and swung across the saddle in front of him while Dawn backed away. With his left hand he gathered his reins, with his right he settled her so she leaned against his shoulder. When she started up to protest she was pulled back again.

"Stay still. You'll startle Nimrod. I'm taking you for that talk I'm due."

"But . . ." she gasped, "what a romantic fashion to do it."

"Romantic nothing. Merely the easiest and quickest way. If I asked you to come you'd have Dawn galloping off in all directions to avoid me. Keep quiet now and figure how you are going to explain yourself."

"I have nothing to explain," she began hotly and raised her head which was firmly returned to place.

"You have. Be still—or you'll annoy me so I won't be able to manage Nimrod who does not like to carry double." The horse was sidling and refusing to trot, so Bourne put him into a long canter towards the woods, then down the ride to the bench by the river. There he tossed the reins over Nimrod's head, slid from the saddle and lifted her down.

"Stand still," he ordered, apparently to both, then picked her up and placed her on the bench, went back and tied Nimrod loosely to a bush which offered good nibbling, and came back and stood before her.

"Now what is this my groom heard last night at the Rose and Crown from one of Deveron's that his lordship has packed and is leaving?" His gray eyes were narrowed and hard. "What games are you playing now?"

So much for secrecy, she thought bitterly, but faced him boldly. "I do not know what you mean. I have never played games, as you have mysteriously accused me. I am not playing one now. Deveron is indeed leaving today."

"And when do you follow him?" he asked harshly.

"Why, I leave in two days, though it is hardly your concern."

"It is. So it's to be a hole-in-the-wall wedding, eh? Where and when?"

"Wedding?" The man was demented. "Another romantic notion, my lord? I know not what you mean."

"I said to stop playing games. The two of you are engaged to be married. I heard you."

"You are quite out of your mind." She was half angry, half bewildered. "You could hear no such thing."

"Why, you little hussy. I heard. And you told me, so happily, you would have a surprise to announce. I forced myself to go to Lady Jersey's to hear. There were the emeralds, true, but that was not the kind of surprise you intimated. Why do you think I went to Gloucestershire but to be absent when it was made?"

"But it *was* only the emeralds, my lord," she began.

"Stop mylording me. It wasn't. I tell you I heard." There was a white line around his mouth and his dark fury was mounting. "And now you're running off together."

Thea took a deep breath. "Sit down, Bourne," and she kept her voice calm. "Tell me what you heard."

Reluctance in every line of his lean figure, he moved slowly to sit at the farthest end of the bench. "You have accused me of so much," she went on, "now explain before I erupt in a fury like your own."

"I am not in a fury, and you have no cause for one except that I have found you out. Very well. Deny it you cannot. It was the morning that Deveron sent for me to ride to London with him and the gold. I came through the woods, left Nimrod by the parterre, and walked up to the windows of the library. It seemed no occasion to be announced. I could hear you two laughing together so gaily. As I came to the open window you were both sitting on the floor and Deveron was saying, 'You are a most endearing girl. My offer stands, you know. Any time. For I do truly love you,' and he kissed you. And you said, 'Dear Myles,' and at that I left for I had no wish to hear, or see, more. Your laughter followed me. Every word has stayed with me. I rode away, then remembered the gold, and returned. That second time . . ." He stopped and turned his head to where the river sparkled through the branches. "As I came that second time, Deveron was saying 'It is a secret for the nonce,' and you said, 'Let us seal the bargain,' and you both shook hands and began to laugh. And what, pray ma'am," he looked back at her sternly, "could any man believe but that you had accepted his hand? And when I remarked that you had everything settled, for I wished to make sure my assumption was correct, you did not contradict me."

"Yes–s–s," she agreed and kicked the skirt of her riding habit and then faced him again. "I can see how a romantic man of violent disposition might leap to that conclusion. But you were sadly wanting in spirit not to inquire in some more direct fashion to confirm your suspicions."

"I am not a romantic man, I say again. And I do not pry out answers no one wishes to give. It was obvious to me."

"Much has been obvious to you that was quite in error, but no matter. I tell you here and now Deveron and I are not marrying."

Instead of looking pleased, as she had hoped, he merely narrowed his eyes again. "Is that merely postponed until he can free himself of Cordelia?"

"Oh, he's done that. He and Gifford are leaving for India."

"And are you going to follow him?" he asked suspiciously. "That would be romantic enough for you, but a nasty voyage for a lone female."

"Again, no. He says he will bring me some sapphires in a year or two."

"Are you relieved of that marrying clause by the discovery of the emeralds? Is it Rushdon you are taking?"

"I am becoming weary of saying no to your questions. Captain Rushdon is rejoining his regiment."

Bourne's eyes were still narrowed in suspicion. "Then

what do you mean you are leaving? To go to whom?"

"No *whom*. No *where*." He was controlling himself so tightly she must lighten this somehow. "Oh, dear," she lowered her eyes and drooped. "We had not thought to tell any of our friends. But I see I must lay it all before you. In two days Ardsley will no longer be mine."

"That is hardly believeable. Go on, tell me." Some of the tautness left him.

At the end of her account he rose. "So having failed in your attempts to attach any gentleman, you are left without a home."

Her head went up. "I never made any effort to attach anyone," she said hotly. "You should know that."

"Oh, not me, I grant you. But others? Well, you had better make sure of a roof over your head and marry me."

"You are insulting." She jumped to her feet. "A cottage would be better than marrying such an odious, domineering, scornful cold-blooded man."

He looked at her at first with amusement, then, with a flash in his eyes, he was beside her. "I'll let you use any adjective you wish, love, but, by Gad, not cold-blooded."

He pulled her to him so quickly she stumbled and was in his arms, and his mouth was on hers, hard and demanding. For a moment she fought his insistence, then found herself yielding. At last he raised his head. "I asked you once before where you learned to kiss," and his voice was uneven. "Tell me now, this instant. Who were they?"

"And I told you in that garden," she flamed. "No one ever kissed me, save on the cheek, but you. You're outrageous again," and tried to push against his chest.

"You're usually truthful. All right. I believe you." He pulled her closer and bent his head and kissed her again until she was lost in wonder at her rush of happiness and then forgot all but this man holding her so implacably and kissing her with his whole being. "There." An exultant note was in his voice when his head rose. "I've wanted to do that since the night by the fountain. This proves we were made for each other. You could never kiss another man that way, nor I another girl. But I'll see you don't get a chance to try."

It was the laughter now in his voice which infuriated her. She made another effort and pushed again. "You are mocking me." She spoke tumultuously for it was hard to breathe evenly. "You said you only kissed me because you were foxed. Are you now? I'll not have that. No, nor pity either. I'm not an object for your charity. I'll not marry you."

He gave her a little shake and let her go so suddenly she had to take hold of his arm. "You're a stupid little witch. Of course, you will. Here, sit down since you can't stand alone, and you look as if you would like to slap me which I will not allow." He picked her up by her elbows and put her down on the bench and placed himself too far away for her to reach.

"I see I will have to explain, which I abhor. The house I offer you is sound and has its attractions and would suit you, though it is not large like the mansion from which you are being ejected. Aunt Erica, I should tell you, is quite enamored of London again and will live there or in Bath. By the way, she told me long ago I would be beyond words stupid if I did not fix my interest with you—and had no patience with my not making that attempt. So the house would be yours to manage as you wish. Once you said you enjoyed that."

Thea took a long breath and found herself quite calm. "You see? You are cold-blooded. What should I care about your house? Yet you offer that as a reason for marrying you."

"No, no. That was merely by the way. But I can't be both cold-blooded and romantic, as you've been telling me."

"Well, you are, and it's deplorable." Her curiosity arose.

"Why did you never pay me attentions?"

He answered seriously. "Never thought of it, at first. You did look like a scrawny waif, and I was sorry for you. But it was also evident you were a girl of spirit, and I began to find myself more interested in you than in any girl I've known. But I knew you were enamored of Deveron from the outset and determined to separate him from Cordelia. I'll not play second string to any man. Then I found I wanted to protect you and take you away from all those around you, which emotion had been unknown to me before. You steadily amused me and I enjoyed all our encounters—a guarantee life with you would never be dull. I began resenting the attentions of other men to you. That night in the garden I was so shaken with jealousy I did not know myself. It took all my powers to restore my usual countenance in your regard and to endeavor to put you from my mind, in which I failed lamentably. But always it seemed evident you and Deveron would make a go of it. I'm not one to allow the world to mark my emotions—the chief reason I left town when I was sure your announcement was imminent."

"Oh." Her eyes widened. "You have said all that so beautifully I cannot believe you. You've admitted, halfway, you've play-acted before. How would I ever know when I could believe you—about me?"

"I'll see you do." His voice had a deeper note. "We'll neither of us have any doubts, love, for I'll never play-act with you again, or give you any cause to suspect me. Once I have you fast, there'll be no need. And even if tempted," and his mouth quirked a little, "I would not dare for you would catch me. You'll always be my enduring delight, you know. But what of you? You must admit you have more than a tendre for me."

"Yes. Perhaps. I don't know. I never let myself think of you, except when I couldn't help it, for you showed you never regarded me with affection. So, like you, I would not let it appear, or admit to myself, that you, you are, are . . ."

The line of the scar deepened as he smiled. "Are what, love? I hope you will come up with a list of adjectives more accurate than your last. You haven't one? Then I'll tell you what you are." His smile now was tender. "Deveron was right. You're the most endearing, darling girl in the world. You're kind and merry and loyal and wholehearted and so lovely in face and person I could spend my life just enjoying the sight of you. You're all the things I most desire and never thought to find in one girl. I love you with absolute desperation, and humbly beg of you to do me the honor of becoming my wife." He moved a little closer. "There. That's the first time I've ever said that. Your turn."

"Bourne, you're the most aggravating man in the world." She jumped up and stamped her foot. "Why, now you expect me to make a declaration. Marrying you would be . . ."

"Yes?" He was standing beside her, not touching her.

"Would be letting you manage me as you have all along—the new clothes, going to London, you even said it would be easier to find a husband here than in town."

"If you'll remember, dear heart, I said to find a meek husband you could manage. You haven't found that."

"And I said I didn't want one such. Oh, I don't know . . . At first I thought Deveron the handsomest man and the most abominable, and you abominable in a different way but sometimes kind. Then he turned friendly and you became more aloof and dictatorial and attractive, particularly when you were being charming. You were so cold at Lady Jersey's I felt you didn't even want to be kind. When you went away, I was sure you didn't care a smidgeon for me, and then I didn't care at all what was happening to me or what I did next. I'd like to believe you but I can't."

"You can and do. You believe me and wish to marry me and let me cherish you with joy all the rest of my life."

"You will . . . ?" she began doubtfully and looked in his eyes and threw herself into his arms. "Oh, Bourne, please do, for I love you to desperation, too, and I couldn't bear to live without you."

"We'll get married tomorrow," he said a little later, somewhat huskily. "We better. I could go on kissing you forever. We must be practical so I can." He lifted his head, looked at her and drew a deep breath. "Don't start saying you'll need brideclothes because you won't, you have all that London wardrobe to take care of you, for a while. I'll get a special license this afternoon. Our parish church is old, simple, always thought I'd like to be married there, if I ever was. I'll send after Deveron, get him here to stand up with me, show him you won't be waiting for those sapphires."

She pulled away a few inches. "There you go, managing everything," she said breathlessly. "Are you always going to be like that?"

"Of course, when you agree. You aren't alone any more, my darling. It's all part of the cherishing I am so going to enjoy."

"Well, I tell you one thing. I will not have you saying Cordelia is to be my attendant."

He threw back his head with a whoop of delighted laughter. "Oh, Thea, I do adore you. No, sweet, I'd not care for that either. Cousin Susan is preferable."

She looked at him, half solemn, half laughing herself. "I think I will like having you manage me after all, when you are reasonable."

"I promise you'll like it. To begin with, you'll sleep this night at Ardsley, and mind you pack everything."

"And?" she asked, suddenly shy.

"Tomorrow you'll be mine. I won't wait any longer. And I'm taking you off to Paris the day after."

"Paris! How wonderful." She clutched the lapels of his jacket. "You mean it? But . . . but I don't need Paris."

"I do, with you. No better place for our honeymoon. I'll show you that. Thea, I can't bear to leave you now, but I must for that special license. But I promise I never will again." And his arms went around her.

Dorothy Eden

Ms. Eden's novels have enthralled millions of readers for many years. Here is your chance to order any or all of her bestselling titles direct by mail.

☐	AN AFTERNOON WALK	23072-4	1.75
☐	DARKWATER	23153-4	1.75
☐	THE HOUSE ON HAY HILL	X2839	1.75
☐	LADY OF MALLOW	23167-4	1.75
☐	THE MARRIAGE CHEST	23032-5	1.50
☐	MELBURY SQUARE	22973-4	1.75
☐	THE MILLIONAIRE'S DAUGHTER	23186-0	1.95
☐	NEVER CALL IT LOVING	23143-7	1.95
☐	RAVENSCROFT	22998-X	1.50
☐	THE SHADOW WIFE	22802-9	1.50
☐	SIEGE IN THE SUN	Q2736	1.50
☐	SLEEP IN THE WOODS	23075-9	1.75
☐	SPEAK TO ME OF LOVE	22735-9	1.75
☐	THE TIME OF THE DRAGON	23059-7	1.95
☐	THE VINES OF YARRABEE	23184-4	1.95
☐	WAITING FOR WILLA	23187-9	1.50
☐	WINTERWOOD	23185-2	1.75

Buy them at your local bookstores or use this handy coupon for ordering:

FAWCETT PUBLICATIONS, P.O. Box 1014, Greenwich Conn. 06830

Please send me the books I have checked above. Orders for less than 5 books must include 60c for the first book and 25c for each additional book to cover mailing and handling. Orders of 5 or more books postage is Free. I enclose $_____ in check or money order.

Mr/Mrs/Miss _____

Address _____

City _____ State/Zip _____

Please allow 4 to 5 weeks for delivery. This offer expires 6/78.

A-5